MASTER OF HOUNDS:
BOOK 1

MASTER OF HOUNDS:
BOOK 1

R. A. STEFFAN

Master of Hounds: Book 1

ISBN: 978-1-955073-15-8 (paperback)

For information, contact the author at
http://www.rasteffan.com/contact/

Cover by Deranged Doctor Design

Second Edition: July 2021

AUTHOR'S NOTE

This book contains descriptions of graphic sex and violence. It is intended for a mature audience.

TABLE OF CONTENTS

ONE

"Throw him to the dogs."

Princep Kaeto, the emperor's son, waved a careless hand toward two guards holding a bound prisoner between them. The pair dragged the unfortunate man forward to the entrance of the royal kennels, where sounds of growling and scrabbling could be heard coming from within.

Caius Oppita, once a respected Legatus of the Alyrion Imperial Guard, stood at parade rest as the order was given, his eyes fixed impassively ahead. Gossip had been rampant in recent weeks concerning the steady parade of prisoners arriving at the royal compound, only to meet inventive and grisly ends on the direct order of the princep. The lithe young man with bound hands and a bag tied over his head was only the latest to confront such an unpleasant fate.

One of the guards addressed the master of hounds, who stood next to the kennel doors, his head bowed in groveling subservience. "Have the beasts been starved for a full week, as His Highness requested?" he asked formally.

The houndsman's shoulders hunched a bit further inward. "Yes—it is as my imperial lord has commanded. They are near-mad with hunger."

The guard nodded. "Then lead the way and hold them off while we toss this piece of garbage into the cage with them."

With a deep breath, the houndsman straightened his spine. He clutched the handle of the whip coiled at his side with a white-knuckled grip, as he entered the low building to complete his unpleasant task. The guards pulled their captive along, following him into the kennel's dark interior. Inside, the ominous growls erupted into full-throated baying, growing in pitch and intensity until the sounds filtering out to Caius and the other observers standing in the courtyard became positively frantic.

Caius fought down a wave of queasiness, not allowing it to show in either his face or his bearing. He'd been a soldier for twenty-nine of his forty-six years... had seen men hacked apart by swords, trampled under the hooves of warhorses, and dying of dysentery in the battle camps. Yet something about this casual cruelty still sickened him. If the talk making the rounds of the palace was accurate—and he had every reason to believe it was—then the only crime committed by the men being executed under Kaeto's hand involved their conception. The wrong seed had reached the wrong womb, resulting in the birth of another inconvenient bastard son.

A few moments later, the guards re-emerged from the kennel. The one who had spoken to the houndsman approached Kaeto and bowed low.

"The master of hounds will stay to watch until the beasts calm enough for whatever remains of the prisoner to be removed," he said, speaking over the din of howling and snarling. "I don't expect they'll leave much behind."

Kaeto made a dismissive gesture. "Let the creatures crack the bones and suck the marrow, for all I care. Leave the filthy whore-son to rot in the manure pile after they shit him out."

Caius continued to stare straight ahead, his expression granite. Stoicism was not enough to prevent him from becoming the next focus of the princep's attention, however.

"You disapprove of my words, Legatus?" Kaeto's voice held amusement, which was somehow even more galling than anger would have been.

I disapprove of your actions, Caius thought. *Not just your words.*

Aloud, he only said, "I prefer witnessing honorable death in battle to death by execution, Your Highness."

The dogs were still in an uproar, though he'd heard no sounds of human screaming. They must've gotten the sad bastard by the throat quickly. At least that would have shortened his suffering, if nothing else.

"Still a soldier to the core, eh?" Kaeto replied. His tone changed, becoming pointed. "Well, if not for certain limitations, of course…" He trailed off, flicking his fingers in the general direction of Caius' twisted left shoulder, where a blow from a battleaxe had mangled the muscles on his dominant side some years ago. "At any rate, Legatus, it's all for the best. I'm certain you've heard the rumors. We can't leave men like that walking around free, now can we?"

"Indeed, Your Highness," he said tonelessly.

Thankfully, Kaeto appeared to lose interest in the exchange when Caius failed to rise to the bait.

"Now," said the princep, turning to address his entourage. "I believe that's quite enough of *that* unpleasantness. Come. Let us return to the palace and see about procuring a meal—preferably one with less gristle than what the dogs are currently enjoying."

Polite titters greeted the tasteless joke.

Kaeto shot Caius a haughty glance. "You. Stay behind. Report to me when the thing is done and the remains disposed of—since that seems to be important to you. One *does* like to have someone they can trust keeping an eye on events."

Caius felt a muscle in his jaw twitch. "As you wish, Your Highness," he replied in a monotone, thinking that from the sound of it, the 'thing' had been done less than a minute after the cage door had slammed closed.

He stood stiffly as the princep, the guards, and the group of fawning courtiers removed themselves from the courtyard, presumably in search of less bloody entertainments. A short time later, he found himself alone except for the houndsman's apprentice—a boy of perhaps twelve or thirteen years of age, with a mop of brown hair and wide gray eyes.

Flies buzzed through air heavy with humidity and the musky smell of animals. With no one but the boy left to see, Caius closed his eyes, feeling the familiar pull of the skin around an old scar bisecting his left eyebrow. The barking inside the kennel had already died down to occasional whines and yips.

His eyes flew open when it unexpectedly erupted again, the sound of baying and growling followed closely by a man's high-pitched shrieks, growing in desperation only to be cut off abruptly. The fine hair on the back of Caius' neck prickled.

What in Deimok's name?

"Go see what's happening," he ordered the boy. It seemed decidedly unlikely that the prisoner could have survived the first round of canine frenzy, but apparently he had. Whatever the case, it sounded as though the unlucky man's time was finally up.

The apprentice gulped nervously and disappeared into the building, only to erupt from the kennel's doorway a few moments later like a cork shot from a bottle of sparkling wine. His face was pale as a sheet as he ran full-pelt across the cobbled yard.

"Sir, come quickly, *please!*" he begged. "It's my master, he's... he's —"

The words choked to a standstill, lodging in his skinny throat. Caius followed with a frown as the boy grasped his sleeve and tugged him in the direction of the cacophony coming from inside the structure. Unsure what he would find, he slipped his ceremonial sword from its sheath right-handed — aware on some level that the weapon would not be enough to fend off an entire pack of crazed hounds, should such a thing become necessary.

Cool shadows enveloped him as he slipped through the door after the boy. Caius blinked rapidly in the kennel's dimly lit interior, straining to see in any detail beyond the mass of dark, milling shapes behind a wall of metal bars. That was something, at least—the cage door was closed, and none of the dogs appeared to be loose. Beside him, the pale apprentice still clutched at Caius' left sleeve, but now the boy's frightened panting had descended into poorly stifled sobs.

Caius tugged his arm free, moving cautiously closer to the bars. As his vision adapted to the low light, he could make out a limp form being jerked to and fro in the middle of the snarling melee. It was vaguely human-shaped... but becoming less so by the second. Again, the feeling of nausea assailed him at the idea of executing someone in such a manner.

He started to turn to the boy, ready to growl at him to explain himself. That was when he noticed two of the hounds fighting over a braided rawhide whip, like pups playing tug-of-war with a length of chewed rope. His brows drew together, and he gave the large area beyond the bars a longer, searching look.

Where was the houndsman?

Now that his eyes had grown accustomed to the dimness, he could make out a second figure hunched in the far corner; back turned to the carnage. It... wasn't the master of hounds.

Dusky skin stretched across lean muscles. The figure appeared to be completely naked. His fingers twined through wild spirals and mats of dark hair, clutching at his own head as though that was the only way he could hold up its weight.

Twisted scars from a long-ago flogging crisscrossed his back.

Caius stood frozen for several moments, attempting to force the tableau into some sort of context. The hounds had left the prisoner untouched — at least beyond ripping away his clothing — and instead savaged their caretaker?

Even now, the animals continued to tear at the corpse, their muzzles coated with gore.

That the houndsman was dead was not in question... and Caius supposed the apprentice's hysteria made sense now. The boy had sunk to the ground behind him, his back pressed to the wall near the door through which they'd entered. He didn't beg Caius to stop what was happening. Any fool could see there was no point in even trying at this late juncture. Instead, the lad merely looked on with unblinking horror as the animals fed on what had, mere minutes ago, been his master.

A living person.

Practicality reared its head. "Is there another whip?" Caius asked. "We should try to get them off the body while there's still something left to bury..."

"No. Let them eat." The raspy voice came from the hunched figure in the back. The prisoner hadn't moved until that moment, but with those words, he let his hands slide free of his hair and looked over his shoulder at Caius. "They're starving. And since I imagine that man was the one who starved them, there's a kind of justice to it, I suppose."

Caius buried the prickle of unease running up his spine. "You. Why aren't you dead?"

The prisoner rose, a bit unsteadily. He seemed either unaware or uncaring of his nakedness as he turned to face Caius and walked toward him.

"I always had a way with dogs," he said. His voice sounded detached. Far away. Around him, the animals parted like water, making way for his passage as he approached the barred door. His chest rose and fell on a deep, unsteady breath. "It's been a while, though. Wasn't sure if I still had the knack or not. Guess I do."

Caius' sense of unease didn't lift, though its flavor shifted incrementally as he became acutely aware of the other man's body. The prisoner stood barely more than arm's length away from him, separated by the heavy iron bars. Caius judged him to be in his mid-twenties, though he looked older than that. Not surprising, after what had probably been years spent languishing in prison for the crime of being born an emperor's illegitimate son.

It was apparent from his skin color and his unusual hair that his mother must have been from one of the southern lands—perhaps Kulawi. His eyes were a rich brown shade, heavy-lidded and accented by dark lashes. His body was hairless except for thatches of black at his armpits and groin. There wasn't an ounce of fat anywhere on his frame, but rather than appearing frail, his arms and legs were corded with lean muscle and sinew.

It was the body of someone who'd been used on the prison work crews rather than kept chained in a cell day in and day out. When he spoke, his accent was provincial, but not unpleasant to the ear.

"So, are you going to kill me now, soldier?" he asked, sounding more tired than fearful. His eyes landed rather pointedly on Caius' drawn sword. Around him, several of the hounds looked up from their grisly meal, and Caius heard the low rumble of warning growls as the beasts sensed the sudden change in atmosphere.

Caius' disquiet over the entire situation coalesced into a sharp, burning point beneath his ribcage. "Do you even know why you're here?" he asked, in lieu of answering the man directly.

The prisoner still looked unutterably weary. "Some nobleman or the other couldn't keep his prick where it belonged, and nine months later, there was me. No clue why someone suddenly decided to turn me into dog meat after ten years of wasting perfectly good food and clothing on me in prison, though."

Caius blinked.

Good god.

The poor bastard didn't even realize who his father was, did he?

An idea both terrible and wonderful in its simplicity percolated through Caius' mind, pushing his heartbeat into a gallop.

"You haven't answered my question," said the prisoner. "Will I die now at your hands, instead becoming food for the pack?"

For a long moment, Caius stood poised on the cusp of what would arguably be an act of treason, wavering. He had watched in silence for the past three years as the empire his family had served for generations slid ever downward, spiraling into corruption and depravity.

The emperor—once a military and organizational genius well on his way to conquering the known world—was losing his wits and his health in equal measure. Of the emperor's three legitimate sons, one was a drunkard, one was a sadist, and one was a manipulative bootlicker. Between them, they threatened to tear Alyrios apart with their power struggles.

And Caius, once a respected general in the Alyrion army, had somehow become the man whose job it was to make sure that the bones of a dead imperial bastard were cleaned up after being devoured by His Highness's hunting dogs.

Almighty Deimok, how had his life come to this?

Twenty-nine years of loyalty and military discipline creaked under the accumulated strain, like rotting timbers on a bridge giving way beneath the force of a flood-swollen river. Caius met the eyes of the man standing on the other side of the bars. The prisoner's gaze was dull with resignation.

"No," he croaked, barely recognizing his own voice. "I'm not going to kill you. Though we may both end up dead if we're not careful."

TWO

The prisoner stared at Caius for a beat before replying, "Sorry, but I can't tell if that's supposed to be reassuring or not. Because if it is, I hate to say it, but you're very bad at reassurance."

"It's not meant as reassurance," Caius said curtly. "It's just the truth. Has anyone inside the palace grounds seen your face?"

The man looked at him like he was trying to peel back Caius' skin so he could examine what lay beneath. "No. The guards who delivered me from the prison kept a bag tied over my head except when they fed me. And I haven't been fed since before I got here. Why?"

Caius ignored the question, his thoughts running fast and hot. "What's your name? Do the guards know it? Does anyone here know it?"

Dark brows drew together in confusion. "It's Decian. And no, they don't. Except for the handful of cellmates who bothered to ask over the years, no one's called me anything except 'prisoner' or 'bastard' since I was sixteen."

This could work, Caius thought, still with no idea why it suddenly seemed so important that it did. *It could work... or it could end up with my neck on a block beneath the executioner's axe.*

"Congratulations, Decian," he said gruffly. "You are now His Imperial Highness's master of

12

hounds—temporarily, at least. You obviously have a knack for the work."

Decian stared at him for a long beat.

"What in the gods' names are you talking about?" he asked slowly.

And... *oh, good*. The emperor's part-Kulawi bastard son was apparently a heretic as well as a perceived threat to the succession. Because *of course* he was.

"There's only one God," Caius said, more sharply than he intended. "And you'll do well to remember it if you want to stay alive in this palace. Now, try to keep up. That sad pile of meat and bone is you—successfully executed, just as Princep Kaeto ordered. However, it appears the houndsman didn't have had the stomach for using his dogs to kill people. He walked off the job right after the deed was done, and promptly disappeared to who knows where. You're his temporary replacement."

"His temporary—?" Decian began, only to cut himself off. He stared at Caius with an incredulous expression. "Seriously... you just decided out of the blue to spare my life, and *this* is your plan?"

Caius' lips twitched into a scowl. "It is until I can get you away from the palace without arousing suspicion. Or... I suppose I could just run you through the heart right now, instead of risking my own position to save the neck of a condemned bastard."

"You think no one's going to notice what an odd coincidence this is?" Decian shot back. "The houndsman disappearing, and a random stranger taking his place?"

Caius' scowl grew. "I think you vastly overestimate the number of people that give a rat's arse about who performs their menial labor for them. No one cares who's tending the dogs, as long as the dogs get tended."

Decian's gaze moved from Caius to the huddled form of the apprentice, who was watching the exchange with wide, red-rimmed eyes. Tear streaks cut through the grime on the lad's cheeks.

Caius sighed.

All right. Perhaps there was at least *one* person who gave a rat's arse.

"You. Boy. Did the houndsman treat you well?" he demanded. "Was he a friend to you?"

The lad's face crumpled for a moment before he steeled himself to speak. "Not really," he said in a tiny voice. "He was a drunkard, and cruel when he'd been at the wine too much. But I didn't... I didn't want..." His gaze wandered toward the bloody mess in the cell, only to jerk away quickly.

"Of course you didn't," Caius said, forcing his voice into something less gruff.

"Did he have a wife?" Decian asked. "A mistress? Children?"

"No," said the apprentice. "I think he went to whores sometimes, though. And he played cards at the Wooly Ram most nights."

Caius cursed himself for not even considering those questions—for assuming that everyone in the world was as alone as he was. Still, the situation should be manageable enough. Prostitutes and gamblers were used to people disappearing as soon as their money dried up.

"Where are his rooms?" he asked, thinking that Decian and the unlucky houndsman were close enough in height and build that the dead man's clothing would probably suffice to replace Decian's shredded prisoner's rags.

"There's a lean-to at the far end of the building," said the boy, still looking on the verge of leaking more tears. "He sleeps there. *Slept* there. I sleep here in the kennel, to watch for thieves." He tipped his chin toward a corner furnished with a stool and a sad little bedroll on the dirt floor.

"All right," Caius said slowly. "Go to the man's room and fetch some of his clothing." He reached awkwardly for the purse hanging at his belt, his bad shoulder giving a warning twinge at the movement. "Here's a silver piece. There will be more if you keep quiet about what you've seen. But if I hear that you've flapped your tongue to anyone, you won't like what happens next."

The child's pale face grew paler, and he gulped audibly. Nonetheless, the coin disappeared quickly into a pouch at the boy's waist, and he hared away without another word. Caius figured he'd either return shortly with clothes, or he'd run for the hills and never be heard from again. The first option was more immediately useful, but he wasn't strictly opposed to the second.

"Do you often threaten children?" Decian asked, once the lad had gone.

"Only the ones who could get me executed with a careless word." Caius threw the other man a hard glance, aware that he would probably be finding this conversation easier to navigate if Decian's cock wasn't hanging out.

The physique of a prisoner who'd spent years breaking rocks and hauling ore had no business looking so appealing—at least from this angle, when they were facing each other and the whip scars on Decian's back were hidden.

"Look—here's a counteroffer," Decian suggested. "Tell me where the nearest palace gate is, and you'll never see or hear from me again."

Caius scowled. "It's not that simple."

Decian scowled back. "Yes it is. All I've ever wanted was to be left the hell alone. Whichever highbred arsehole sired me, they've got nothing to worry about from me. The *last* thing I want is more attention."

Caius' jaw was growing sore from how hard he was clenching it. "Believe me, I'd like nothing better than to send you on your merry way. But if there's one shredded body, no houndsman, and no prisoner, suddenly this farce becomes a *mystery*. There would be an investigation."

"Let them investigate," Decian said tiredly.

"On top of that," Caius continued, "since the guards at the gates won't recognize you, they're as likely to arrest you as let you through. Access into and out of this place is tightly controlled—unless you know the guards personally, you'll be subject to scrutiny you don't want. A lot of the laborers in the palace compound are slaves—escape attempts aren't uncommon."

Decian's eyes narrowed. "And my skin color makes me look like a slave, does it?"

Caius shrugged. "Not really. It does make you stand out, though. Slaves are as likely to be Alyrion as foreign, and I've known plenty of freemen from Kulawi and the southern reaches. But none of that will help you if the guards at the gate start asking the wrong questions."

The younger man subsided, though he still looked unhappy. Small surprise there, Caius supposed. After all, he *was* locked in a cage with a pack of starving dogs busily consuming a human corpse, and Caius had just told him he'd have to stay in the palace compound with his would-be executioners for an unspecified amount of time.

"It should only be for a few days," he offered. "Spin some story about being an acquaintance of the houndsman. Tell anyone who asks that he suggested you take the job before he left. Once the guards learn your face and your story, head into the city for some evening entertainment and keep going. Get as far away from Amarius as you can and never look back."

Decian stared at him with a piercing gaze the color of rich, freshly turned earth. He lifted his chin, and the weak light filtering in from the doorway caught his eyes oddly for an instant, making them almost seem to glow.

"Why are you doing this?" he asked. "Why put yourself at risk for a condemned man?"

Honesty tugged at Caius, drawing out words better left unsaid. "Because I no longer recognize my own country. Alyrios should not be a place where men are thrown to ravenous dogs because of the circumstances of their birth. It's wrong. This is not the empire I pledged to serve."

There are a number of dead bastards who probably wish you'd reached that conclusion a bit sooner, observed a razor-sharp little voice in the back of Caius' mind.

Decian still watched him with that oddly penetrating gaze. "So this is your grand act of rebellion, is it?" Silence stretched for an uncomfortable beat before he shrugged, snapping the tension. "Fine, I'll take it. It's certainly better than the alternative."

Caius' attention slid toward a pair of hounds snarling over what was probably a thighbone. "I should think so, yes."

The boy chose that moment to return, creeping through the door with a bundle of clothing under his arm.

"Clothes! Well, thank the gods for that," Decian said, apparently oblivious to his recurring blasphemy.

Caius swallowed a growl of frustration, along with the growing concern that he'd just made the worst mistake of his life.

"Is the cage door locked?" he asked gruffly.

"I don't think so," Decian said. "Though I suppose if I'm to be the new master of hounds, I'll still need the keys."

He looked around the cage, his attention landing on the floor near a handful of dogs tearing at a nearly bare ribcage. He walked over without hesitation and shoved the animals off. All but one slunk away. The holdout gave a low growl of warning, teeth clamped around its prize.

"Oh, *hush*," Decian said, glaring down at it for the space of a couple of heartbeats. "Let me get the damned key ring and you can go back to your meal in a minute."

Caius held his breath, but the standoff broke abruptly and without drama a moment later. The massive hound whimpered and dropped the hunk of human torso, crawling away on its belly. Decian stepped forward and picked up a jangling metal ring of keys, giving it a brisk shake to dislodge bits of gore.

Only when he turned and headed away did the animals cautiously return to the bones, watching him warily as he moved off. There was a low trough of water along one side of the cage. Decian sloshed the key ring in it and returned to the cage door.

He paused with his hand on one of the iron bars. "No second thoughts about running me through with your sword and saving yourself the trouble?"

"Several, actually," Caius said truthfully. "So don't try my patience. Get out here and get some damned clothes on, assuming you can do so without any of the dogs getting loose."

Decian scoffed, pushing a couple of hounds out of the way with his leg. They made no attempt to bury sharp teeth into the offending appendage. Caius experienced another sharp flash of disquiet over his abrupt loss of sanity as Decian eased the door open and slipped out, leaving the dogs huddled meekly inside their cage.

Distantly, Caius remembered a young man in the village where he'd grown up who'd seemed to have an almost uncanny affinity for horses. Perhaps he was seeing a similar talent now, but with dogs. The dead houndsman had been a diffident, beaten-down figure. If nothing else, Decian's frankly bizarre fearlessness in the face of the slavering beasts probably worked in his favor.

Decian took the bundle of clothes from the red-faced apprentice, who was still watching both of them with wide eyes. Caius felt the tension in his shoulders ease incrementally as he pulled on a pair of trousers and a shirt — as though Decian's nakedness were truly his most pressing problem right now.

"Right," Decian said, as he straightened from pulling on the dead man's spare boots. "What's your name, lad?"

"Everyone calls me Pip," the apprentice mumbled.

"Great," Decian said. "So, Pip — why don't you show me where the meat for the dogs is kept?" His eyes slid to Caius and held. "And once they've been fed properly, *you* can help me gather up the *unfortunate prisoner's* remains." A sharp-edged smile drew Decian's full lips back, baring white teeth.

It wasn't a pleasant expression, and it shouldn't have felt like a dagger sliding painlessly home below Caius' ribcage, spreading heat in its wake. He cleared his throat. Under the circumstances, Caius supposed he couldn't exactly order anyone else to clear away the bones. Not unless he wanted that person asking the wrong kind of questions—specifically, questions that had no good answers.

"Oh, good," he replied without enthusiasm. "What a coincidence. That's *exactly* how I'd hoped to spend my evening."

THREE

Hours later, Caius returned to the palace to offer a succinct report on the prisoner's supposed death. A brief visit to his quarters followed, and now he lay sprawled on a comfortable divan in Saleene's suite of rooms. He'd bathed and changed before coming to the brothel, wanting very badly to divest himself of all reminders of his recent, abrupt descent into insanity.

Well... that, along with the smell of blood and dog shit.

If nothing else, showing up at Saleene's door while reeking like an abattoir would have been unforgivably rude—and there were not so many prostitutes in the city of Amarius who catered to Caius' tastes that he could afford to piss her off for no reason.

Saleene blinked up at him with kohl-lined eyes from her position between his thighs, her lips sliding along his length in a slow, firm glide. Two blunt-tipped fingers had also been crooked inside him for some time now, rubbing firmly. Caius was aware of his pleasure rising—but distantly, as though it were happening to someone else.

His mind was stubbornly elsewhere, but after a slow, protracted buildup, the sensation eventually peaked. When it did, he spent over

Saleene's tongue with a shudder, his eyes sliding shut as some of the tension flowed out of his body in tandem with his seed.

She pulled off his softening prick with an obscene pop, sliding her fingers free at the same time. Caius swallowed a grunt of discontent at the sudden feeling of emptiness, slinging his good arm across his face to block out the low light of the oil lamp. He was aware of Saleene rising from her place between his thighs to clean up, returning a few moments later to perch on the end of the divan.

"My, my," she began in her familiar low tenor. "You know, I'm not sure I've ever seen a man less interested in the fact that his cock was being sucked. Deep thoughts tonight, *Legatus*?"

The undertone of mockery behind the military title was nothing new, but it was nevertheless unwelcome right now. Caius lowered his arm to shoot her an unimpressed look. She didn't back down from it, tossing her thick mane of wavy black hair over her shoulder. Square-jawed and broad-shouldered, Saleene was a study in contrasts. Her sharp cheekbones were dusted with rouge, and her thin lips were painted red—smudged, now, after her slow and underappreciated seduction of Caius' prick. Her bearing was sultry and inescapably feminine. But her chest was flat muscle beneath the artfully draped folds of her dress, and Caius was more than passingly familiar with the thick length hanging between her legs. It was a cockstand that could, for the right amount of money, take someone apart from the inside out.

In a society where the exposure of homosexual liaisons could ruin a man, Saleene had carved out a niche providing a very particular service, shielded behind a veil of plausible deniability. Caius—whose interest in soft thighs and yielding bosoms had waned significantly after his wife's death in childbirth many years ago—found Saleene's services decidedly to his tastes these days.

Tonight, though, such a diversion still failed to distract him from his own idiocy.

"I'm a fool, Saleene," he said, because in the end, if a man couldn't unburden himself to his favorite prostitute, what had the world come to, really?

"Oh, yes?" she replied in a noncommittal tone. "Have you behaved foolishly, then?"

"Almost certainly," he told her with a sigh, letting his head fall back to stare at the beams in the ceiling. "I tried to right an injustice."

"And trying to right injustice makes one a fool?" Saleene asked. "I think I must've missed that part."

"Not universally, no. But in this case, the attempt amounted to treason," he explained, wondering for the dozenth time what in heaven's name had possessed him.

He felt Saleene shift on the other end of the divan, as though leaning forward in interest. "Treason? Really? And do you regret serving the cause of treasonous justice?"

He closed his eyes again, attempting to banish the vision of Decian's blank look of shock when he realized he'd just been offered a chance at survival.

At *freedom*, if he could hold out for a few days without being discovered.

"That remains to be seen," he admitted.

"Hmm," Saleene said.

She rose again, a clink of goblets signifying the imminent offer of wine. It wasn't kindness; Caius would be paying for the drink and the sympathetic ear right along with the sex. Perhaps it was pathetic of him. However, the alternative was to be utterly alone in the pit of vipers that made up the Alyrion royal court. Most days, Caius felt as though he fit in amongst the schemers and the arselickers of Amarius about as well as an aging carthorse fit in during a chariot race.

He supposed it was surprising that he'd lasted as long as he had without buckling. Maybe the events of this afternoon—or something like them—had been inevitable.

Saleene nudged his hip with her knee to get his attention and pressed a goblet into his unresisting hand. He transferred it from left to right and sipped. Meanwhile, she eased herself to sit on the thick fur rug, resting her back against the front of the divan with her skirts spread out before her.

"The city is rife with talk of the upcoming Council, you know," she said conversationally, as though they were resuming a previous discussion. "It takes up more and more of the conversation every day."

He grunted, not sure what he was expected to say to such an opening gambit.

The Council of Amarius had been called in response to the growing tension between the followers of Deimok and the pagan holdouts who still insisted on following the old ways, even though the emperor himself had declared Deimonism the true religion of the Alyrion Empire. It was no wonder the city was speaking of little else in the run-up.

"At least once the Council rules, things will finally be decided," Caius offered. For all that he had more reason than most to distrust pagans and their dark magic, he had limited interest in—or patience for—religion in general. He kept to the form of the thing... performed the religious duties expected of a respectable advisor to the emperor, and didn't give it much thought beyond that. He found ideologues on either side more than a little incomprehensible.

"*Decided*, yes," Saleene echoed in a tart tone. "And then we shall see whether the zealots who believe it's the Church's duty to execute pagan heretics will hold sway over the moderates who prefer to leave such punishment in Deimok's hands."

Caius raised an eyebrow at her and took another sip of his wine. "You have opinions on the matter, I take it?"

Saleene snorted. "Everyone in the damned city has opinions, my dear Legatus." She lifted her chin, regarding him with a level gaze. "I did have a point to the observation, however."

"Oh?" he asked blankly.

She sighed. "The point is, Caius, that change is coming, and when it arrives, it won't be gentle. You're an advisor to the emperor and his family.

Like it or not, you'll eventually have to pick a side in the endless skirmishes between factions, rather than continuing to play both ends against the middle."

Caius stiffened, the barb hitting home with perhaps more force than Saleene had intended.

"I don't know what you mean," he said, swinging his legs over the opposite side of the divan and rising abruptly. He set his goblet on a side table before moving to retrieve his clothing. Saleene watched him with an impassive gaze as he pulled on his smallclothes, stockings, and breeches, not commenting on the awkward double shoulder-shrug required to get his linen shirt over the ugly twist of scar tissue that limited the range of motion of his left arm.

He was lying, of course—to Saleene, and probably to himself as well. He knew exactly what she meant, though it bothered him that he'd apparently become so transparent. Over the years, Caius had come to despise the royal family he was sworn to serve—but rather than do anything about it, he merely seethed silently over the slow collapse of the empire he loved while corruption unfolded around him, unchecked.

At least, he had done nothing about it until today.

Today, he'd taken action to try to save a single life... yet even in this, he'd only been moved to act after the fact. He'd stood at parade rest while an innocent bastard had been thrown, quite literally, to the dogs... and he'd stayed silent. Only when Kaeto had retired with his cadre of fawning sycophants, and the dogs had miraculously spared their intended victim, had Caius stepped up to the task of seeing justice done.

Taking only what action could be achieved with minimal risk.

Playing both ends against the middle.

"It's late. I must return to the palace," he said, the words clipped. He fumbled in his coin purse for payment, tossing the money onto the table next to the wine.

Another whore might have scrambled to smooth her client's ruffled feathers, but Saleene only watched him pull on his boots with a neutral expression. Caius held no illusions regarding their relationship—not in this regard, anyway. Saleene might appreciate him as a man who paid well and gave no trouble, but should he walk out of her brothel and never return, there would be a dozen other men lining up to take his place.

Besides, he would be back within a fortnight when the pall of loneliness once more grew too stifling. They both knew it. None of which changed the fact that he was in no mood to appreciate having his very palpable shortcomings thrown in his face tonight, either intentionally or unintentionally.

He left her suite without another word, heading down the stairs to retrieve his sword belt from a little room off the main receiving parlor, where the clients' weapons were held for safety. He'd made it roughly halfway down when the sound of raised voices reached him from below. A low growl of irritation from the room he'd just left alerted him to Saleene's rapid approach behind him. She brushed past him on the stairwell, all lean grace, her skirts held up with one hand.

When Caius arrived a few moments later, it was to find a four-way standoff in the brothel's parlor. Saleene and her partner Zuri—a dark-skinned Kulawi woman with a ready smile and a vicious temper—formed two corners of the square. The richly dressed woman forming the third corner was a stranger to him, but Caius vaguely recognized the young man who seemed to be the target of the others' ire.

He was attached to the brothel in some capacity... a lad of perhaps nineteen with a face too pretty for his own good. Caius didn't know his name, but he'd occasionally been the one to take Caius' weapons before he went upstairs to Saleene's rooms. He had the sense that the lad was well aware of his good looks and had a rather high opinion of himself.

Having no interest in whatever sordid incident had precipitated the argument, Caius averted his eyes from the group as the rich woman gestured at the young man angrily. By the time he'd retrieved his sword belt from the wide-eyed girl in charge of watching over the patrons' belongings tonight, the finely dressed female client had stormed out, leaving through the tavern that fronted the street.

As he moved to follow suit, however, he couldn't help overhearing Saleene's hissed, "I told you, Tullio, *one* more angry noblewoman and you're out on your ear—" followed by the lad's querulous words of self-defense. Caius let the door swing shut behind him, heading through the busy tavern. Rather than leaving through the main entrance, he made his way to a back door leading into an alleyway that would, in turn, take him to the main *vaia* running north toward the palace complex.

The scuff of a boot against cobblestone in the dimly lit alley made him pause and look back. A cloaked figure in the shadows froze in place. Caius stared at the man for the space of a handful of heartbeats before dismissing the oddness of the moment and continuing toward the busy road ahead.

Amarius was not enemy territory. There were no scouts hiding in the shadows, waiting to spring an ambush. No doubt the man had merely been a drunkard stepping out behind the tavern for a few moments, surprised to find he didn't have the privacy he'd expected for a quick piss.

Caius put the momentary flash of disquiet from his mind. Tomorrow, he would once more have to face his duties, while also checking that Decian hadn't done anything foolish and drawn attention to himself. Tonight, however, there was a bottle of strong brandy in his rooms that very much had his name on it.

FOUR

The following morning, Caius stood at attention in an echoing meeting chamber near the heart of the palace. Dressed impeccably as befitted his rank, he was surrounded by opulence and excess as he waited for the assembly to come to order. He couldn't think of anyplace he less wanted to be.

Proclus was late. *Again.* It was anyone's guess whether the emperor's eldest son would bother to make an appearance at all. He was probably passed out drunk in his bedroom, drooling all over a naked serving girl or three. Caius wondered if anyone had been sent to wake him. Perhaps Bruccias had gone to get him, since the youngest son, too, was conspicuous by his absence.

That left sharp-eyed Kaeto seated at his father's left hand. As was often the case these days, the Emperor Constanzus seemed distracted, his attention on something in the middle distance that only he could see. The courtiers and advisors in attendance at the day's meeting buzzed among themselves, speaking of the latest gossip. Here, too, all attention was focused on the upcoming ecumenical council.

For all that he hated politics and religious wrangling, Caius was no fool. There were undercurrents roiling in the city, beyond the very real questions surrounding the continued practice of paganism within the empire. Those undercurrents were doubtless at least part of the reason Caius had attended more than a dozen grisly executions of royal bastards in recent weeks. It was also the reason Princep Kaeto had been front and center at every meeting and advisory session since the conclave was first announced.

With no valid path to the throne unless his elder brother conveniently decided to choke to death on his own vomit during a drunken fit, Kaeto sought to gain influence and support among the clergy by exhibiting the kind of leadership that his father and brother weren't.

It was not, in the end, a terrible strategy.

Caius had no desire to serve a wine-swilling fool as the ruler of an empire spanning a quarter of the known world. He had even *less* desire to serve a poisonous sadist in that same role. As things stood now, they'd be lucky to avoid a civil war on the way to either one of those options.

The doors of the chamber swung open and the herald entered, staff in hand. "Your Imperial Majesty, I present to you Episkopos Philian of Narvonne!"

Caius swallowed a sigh. Philian was a high-ranking member of the Church—a thin-featured older man with a silver tongue that was probably forked like a serpent's. With his arrival, any hope of a quiet and productive meeting fled.

The episkopos stopped before the massive table dominating the room and bowed perfunctorily to the royals at its head. Several of the courtiers bowed to him in turn. Caius did not join them, trusting that his military garb would make him functionally invisible to the churchman—a nameless guard rather than the trusted advisor he allegedly was. It wasn't a stretch. He might have saved the emperor's life once upon a time, but these days there seemed to be little enough interest in his counsel.

"Emperor Constanzus," Philian began, "I have come today to enjoin you to better control the rabble in the capital. You may be unaware of this, but there are reports of pagan heretics marching openly in the streets after dark. With the date of the conclave approaching, I'm sure I don't have to tell you how inflammatory such unrest appears to an outside observer."

The emperor frowned in evident confusion, tapping his fingertips restlessly on the marble tabletop as silence stretched. As ever when confronted with the stark changes between the man he had once followed into battle and the fading shell before him, Caius felt his stomach twist. Constanzus was roughly the same age as Caius, and yet his mind was visibly failing week by week.

Kaeto stepped in before the pause could grow any more uncomfortable than it already was. "His Imperial Majesty appreciates your report, Episkopos Philian. This is yet more proof that the heretics lack respect for their rulers, both secular and spiritual."

Philian looked mollified, though his eyes flicked to Constanzus briefly. "I trust the issue will be addressed in a satisfactory manner before the Council convenes." He hesitated, his eyes sweeping the figures at the head of the table. "Forgive me, but... is Princep Proclus well? I would have expected him to be present this morning."

"My brother is indisposed, I fear," Kaeto said evenly, allowing the barest hint of disapproval to color the words.

"Yes," Constanzus echoed in a tone of distraction. "Indisposed."

With a mere handful of words, the emperor's middle son had drawn attention to the fact that his father was slipping and his elder brother was unreliable. Caius might have been impressed, if Kaeto weren't such a damned viper.

"Indeed," Philian said, and his expression grew speculative. "Well, thank you for hearing my concerns, Your Majesties. My secretary will convey the latest details regarding the preparations this afternoon."

He bowed again, clearly preparing to leave, but the emperor straightened in his chair.

"Do you enjoy the hunt, Philian?" Constanzus asked, his gaze clearing.

Philian blinked. "I... beg your pardon, Your Imperial Majesty?"

"The hunt," Constanzus repeated. "Do you enjoy riding to the hounds?"

Caius twitched at the mention of *hounds*. He couldn't help it.

The episkopos merely looked confused. "I fear I have never hunted, Emperor Constanzus."

"What, never?" the emperor replied in disbelief. "Why, we must remedy this immediately! Caius"—he gestured Caius forward—"organize a royal hunt for two days hence! I tire of this endless nattering across tables."

A sinking feeling took up residence in Caius' stomach. He hesitated for the space of a heartbeat, in hopes that Kaeto would step in and redirect his father's attention to more pressing matters before the order stuck and became real.

It was a vain hope. Kaeto was all in favor of anything that highlighted the emperor's growing mental confusion. The princep merely looked on impassively.

Caius cleared his throat. "Of course, Your Imperial Majesty. I will see to it."

Dear god. A hunt. In two days. A hunt... *using the royal hounds.*

The houndsman was dead, and an imposter now ran the kennels. Decian wouldn't have the first idea how to manage the pack during such an outing.

It was all Caius could do to keep one ear on the meeting as Philian left and talk turned to preparations for the arrival of the remaining Church dignitaries. The advisors droned on, and he managed to answer a couple of basic questions about security around the site of the conclave.

The only saving grace was that the emperor's order gave him a perfect excuse to speak with Decian privately. He'd been struggling to think of a reason why a military advisor to the emperor's family would be rubbing shoulders with someone so far below him in station. Now he had one.

The interminable palaver finally wound down. Caius neatly avoided the two courtiers who tried to draw him into conversation about the emperor's obvious befuddlement, and another who accosted him with questions about Proclus' whereabouts. As much as he wanted to flee straight to the kennels and attempt to determine how badly fucked they were going to be, there were other duties that also required his attention.

He made himself take a deep, centering breath, and headed toward the training grounds at the north end of the palace compound. There, he found Aelio drilling the men who were not on guard duty that day — running them through intricate sword forms in the bright sunlight.

"Tribuni," Caius called, once he was in hailing distance.

The Amarian commander looked up, and immediately spoke to the subordinate standing next to him. The soldier smoothly took over the drills, while Aelio crossed to meet Caius halfway.

"Good morning, Legatus," the tribuni greeted. "Escaped from the palace already? Surely that bodes well for the day."

Aelio was a good-tempered fellow — blue-eyed and sandy-haired, with a glint of humor that tended to surface often and easily. Were Caius inclined to make friends of subordinates, he might have considered that Aelio would be an agreeable drinking companion. Since he was not thus inclined, he contented himself with the pleasure of not being constantly at odds with a disobliging palace commander.

"Every day has its own set of problems," he replied, by way of greeting. "I need to discuss the upcoming guard assignments for the arriving Council members. It may be necessary to requisition additional men from the Amarian Guard."

To his credit, Aelio immediately fell to business. "I see. Does this mean we're expecting a degree of trouble beyond the scope of your common- or garden-variety security detail?"

Caius' felt his expression settle into hard, unhappy lines. "These days, I expect little else besides trouble."

Aelio nodded. "Understandable, considering the growing unrest in the city. Very well, I will send a message to Laurentin and advise him that we'll be needing some of his troops. I'm sure *that* will go over well."

"I don't care if he likes it. I just need him to do it," Caius replied.

"Then you will probably be in luck, on both counts," Aelio said solemnly. "Now, while you're here, do you have a few minutes to go over the disposition of the palace troops during the talks? I have some questions about the best placement of the household guard, since I have a feeling Princep Kaeto will be spending more time at the Council than in the palace…"

Caius joined Aelio under the awning abutting the practice field to hammer out a usable plan for the coming weeks, knowing that the situation would be subject to change depending on the progression of the pagan unrest. It was a relief to deal with someone competent and plain speaking after time spent in the company of royals, churchmen, and courtiers. Nonetheless, once the main points had been addressed to both their satisfaction, Caius prepared himself to play the role he was ill equipped to play.

"I don't suppose you've met the new master of hounds?" he asked, striving for a casual tone, and feeling ridiculous.

Aelio appeared taken aback. Not surprising, since Caius wasn't prone to either gossip or personal conversations.

"Er… no. I wasn't aware there *was* a new master of hounds. What happened to the old master of hounds?"

"Walked off the job, I gather," Caius said. "Though he did have the good grace to bring on an acquaintance to take his place when he left. The emperor has ordered a hunt in two days. I'm on my way to speak with the new man next."

The seed was planted. Caius was loath to get further into it, for fear of the conversation coming across as completely out of character.

Aelio's face took on the same look of disbelieving bewilderment that Caius suspected he had worn upon receiving the orders. "A… hunt?" he echoed. "*Now*?" The tribuni ran a hand over his face. "By the One God… he's getting worse, isn't he?"

Such an utterance was dangerously close to treasonous — not that Caius held the moral high ground regarding such things these days.

"His Imperial Majesty's priorities are perhaps different from ours," he replied carefully. How he hated this cautious verbal dance. This sense that speaking plainly was akin to signing one's own death warrant.

"That's putting it mildly," Aelio muttered, apparently less concerned with the dance than Caius was.

"Be prudent with your words," he warned, less harshly than he probably should have. "The emperor commands. We obey. I must leave now for my meeting with the houndsman. I'll let you know by tonight what sort of security we'll be needing for the royal hunting party."

"Of course, Legatus," Aelio replied, once more the picture of professionalism. "Our lives are ever at the emperor's disposal."

Aren't they just, Caius thought, as he nodded and took his leave.

40

FIVE

Decian was easy enough to find, playing dice with a group of workmen in the same courtyard where he'd been dragged in as a condemned prisoner a mere day before. A number of hounds lolled around the little group—tongues hanging out, sunning themselves contentedly. Caius gave them a wary look as he approached.

He was halfway across the yard when one of the men noticed him and straightened abruptly from the game. "Legatus," he said, bowing stiffly as his companions looked up and quickly followed suit. All but Decian, seated facing away from him, who straightened but did not crane around to look.

He'd cut his hair. The wild mats and spirals were gone, leaving tight black curls hugging his head like a sleek helmet.

"I need to speak to the new houndsman," Caius told the others. "Return to your duties."

The men scattered, leaving him alone with Decian and the lazing dogs. The day was balmy, the air carrying the scent of animals. Decian finally turned and met Caius' eyes.

"I was winning before you interrupted that game, you know," he said mildly. "And wasn't it you who told me to make friends with the men in the palace?"

The strange sense of unease from yesterday had returned to Caius' chest within moments of arriving in Decian's presence. He forced it aside. "I'm not sure taking their coin is the best way to make friends with them. Where did you even get money to gamble?"

Decian raised an eyebrow. "I inherited a coin purse that had been stuffed inside my predecessor's palliasse. Pip and I split the contents, since it's not as though dear old Jona is going to need money now that he's moved to greener pastures... so to speak."

"So, the lad stuck around, then?" Caius asked, surprised. Though maybe he shouldn't have been — between the bribe Caius had given him and his share of the spoils in the coin purse, Pip was on course to become the highest paid houndsman's apprentice in all of Alyrios.

"He did, yes," Decian confirmed, stretching a hand out to scratch the ears of the nearest dog. "So, it turns out you're not just any old soldier. You're a *Legatus*, of all things. Tell me — what can I do for you today?"

It occurred to Caius that he hadn't introduced himself at all during their previous interaction... not even to the extent of offering his rank. An instant later, he decided that was probably for the best, under the circumstances. The fewer personal details Decian knew about him, the better.

"The emperor has ordered a royal hunt the day after tomorrow," he said simply. "Given your... recent introduction to this role, is that going to be a problem?"

Decian blinked at him. "That's a good question," he said after a short pause. He lifted his voice. "*Oy, Pip!*"

The apprentice stuck his head out of the door to the kennels and jogged toward them a moment later. Caius saw the boy's face go pale as he recognized him.

"Yes, Decian?" he asked, flicking a worried look in Caius' direction.

"There's going to be a hunt in two days," Decian told him. "Do you know what that entails?"

Pip swallowed. "Y-yes, sir. I've been on four hunts, helping out with Jo—" He trailed off, his gaze slipping to his feet. "With... the old master of hounds."

Decian shrugged. "That's good enough for me. You can talk me through it between now and then."

One of the hounds rolled onto its back, and Pip reached down absently to rub its belly. None of the beasts looked remotely ready to take down a boar or a hart. Nor did they look remotely like the kind of animals that could tear a man limb from limb— which only proved that appearances could be deceiving.

"So... a hunt." Decian looked speculative. "Which, presumably, takes place outside the palace grounds. Somewhere remote, I'm guessing?"

Caius heard the question he wasn't asking. "Yes. This will be your chance to slip away and never look back—assuming your apprentice here can get the pack back to the kennel on his own, without anyone getting bitten." He raised a pointed eyebrow at the lad.

Pip looked offended, his earlier nervousness forgotten. "Of course I can!" he snapped, and quickly added, "*sir*."

Decian snorted in wry amusement at the near-slip.

Caius held Pip's gaze, frowning. "You're not afraid of the dogs after what you saw yesterday?"

A hint of mulish anger hardened the boy's face. "*I* know better than to starve them for a week, no matter what some *nobleman* says."

"Good lad," Caius and Decian said, practically in unison.

Decian gave another small huff of amusement. "It's settled, then. Two more days and I'll be on my way. Now, if that's all, *Legatus* — why don't you get out of here so I can focus on learning all about royal hunts?"

The casual dismissal shocked Caius for a moment. But why should it? His rank meant nothing to Decian. As far as Decian was concerned, Caius was the crazy soldier who had disobeyed orders to save him — nothing more. All Decian wanted was to be far away from here, alive and free from imprisonment. Now that a path to freedom was almost within his grasp, that would become his whole focus, just as it should be.

As it should be for *both* of them.

"Very well, then. A fair afternoon to you both," Caius said, and left him to it.

>⌒⌒ ⚜ ⌒⌒<

The following day passed in a flurry of meetings, along with frantic scurrying to reschedule the important things that had been preempted by the upcoming hunt. By nightfall, Caius was twice as exhausted by the endless palaver as he would have been after riding with the hounds for half a day. He fell into his bed with a vaguely directed prayer for uninterrupted sleep. Instead, he dreamed.

He was in the forest, searching. Warm brown eyes set in a dusky-skinned face beckoned him forward silently before slipping out of view behind the bole of a massive tree. Caius followed, steadying himself with a small hand against the rough bark, dampened by humidity.

A child's hand.

It was too quiet — no birds chirped, rustling leaves with their flight. No dapples of ever-shifting sunlight reached the layer of decaying leaves at his feet. Caius circled the tree trunk, but the lithe figure with the deep brown eyes was already gone, disappearing behind another tree perhaps ten paces away. Caius crashed through the leaf litter in pursuit, his sandaled footsteps shockingly loud in the muffling silence. Always, his quarry remained just at the edge of vision. A glimpse here, a flicker of movement there — nothing more.

Eventually, a clearing opened ahead of him, and Caius stumbled to a halt. Gray clouds choked the sky, except for a single patch of brilliant blue. A narrow beam of yellow sunlight illuminated the trampled grass at the edge of the clearing, broken stalks painted red. A great stag lay crumpled on the ground. Its antlers jutted up like the bare limbs of a dying tree, crimson at the tips. Stripes and splatters of red crisscrossed its tawny coat, three spears jutting obscenely from its body. Its tongue lolled from its open mouth, swollen and dark purple with trapped blood.

Caius didn't want to look at the shapes arrayed around it on the ground. If he looked, it would be real. No, no, no, he chanted, with a child's desperate hope that wishing for something with enough conviction could make it true. His dream legs moved without his command, one in front of the other, bringing him forward until the splayed shapes around the fallen stag became men.

No, he thought again, but it didn't make any difference. His feet continued to propel him closer, until he was standing over the nearest man. A familiar face stared up at the sky sightlessly. His father's expression had frozen into lines of horror. Sticky blood trailed from a rip in the side of his throat to a puddle drying on the ground. His blade was still clasped in one hand, his fingers gripping the hilt like claws.

In the next moment, Caius felt himself falling, tumbling down into a dark pit of boyhood terrors. He tore his eyes away from the body of the man who'd bounced him on his knee as a babe and played at wooden swords with him, looking instead at the stag. It stared back at him with dead eyes, pinning him in place. Caius caught his breath as a blood-red glimmer began to kindle in the depths of those dark orbs, growing until the scarlet glow spilled from them like torchlight.

Horror caught him in the chest like a kick from a mule. He cried out, staggering backward—

—and woke abruptly, jolting upright in bed. His bad shoulder flared with pain at the sudden movement. Sweat beaded his brow. His heart hammered, the breath in his lungs coming fast and shallow. Beyond the open window, the stars twinkled down at him mockingly.

It had been years since the childhood nightmare had plagued him in such a way. His father had been a guardsman in the administrative district encompassing the village where Caius had grown up. Even four decades ago, reports of pagan shapeshifters had grown rare within the empire's borders, as most of the warlocks who could transform into dangerous beasts had already been hunted down.

Rare... but not unheard of.

When the elders in his village accused a man of transforming into a stag and damaging the crops, Caius' father and two of his comrades had been sent to hunt him down and determine the truth of the allegation. Instead, they'd been gored to death by a murderous supernatural creature. Caius — eight years old at the time — had snuck after his father that morning, in hopes of witnessing what he'd childishly assumed would be a grand adventure. Instead, he'd become lost in the woods during the chase, unable to regain his bearings as the sound of screaming echoed through the distant trees. He'd eventually stumbled across the blood-soaked bodies at the edge of a clearing.

As a youngster, he'd revisited that horror in the form of frequent night terrors, though they'd gradually faded as he grew older.

He shook his head, trying to clear it. No doubt it was all the talk of pagans surrounding the upcoming Council that had dredged up memories better left buried. Caius cautiously eased himself down to lie flat on the mattress once more, grimacing at the sensation of damp sweat cooling on the sheets. Blinking up at the darkness, he silently chastised himself for letting the current situation get to him.

It was ridiculous to lose sleep over such things, when there were far more tangible and immediate threats to be dealt with. He closed his eyes and forced his breathing to slow, intent on getting enough sleep so that he wouldn't be totally useless the next day.

SIX

Morning came far too soon after a night spent tossing and turning restlessly. Nevertheless, Caius was ready and waiting on horseback in the main courtyard before the sun breached the eastern wall of the Amarian imperial quarter. A hunt, it turned out, was one of the few things that could rouse the royal household before dawn, drawing them from their comfortable beds with the promise of excitement and the glory of the kill.

Even Proclus had managed to overcome his hangover, appearing bleary-eyed and snappish, laced into his clothing and hoisted onto a mount by his small army of servants. Sharp-eyed Kaeto was there as well, of course, and the youngest—Bruccius—skulked in the background on a round-barreled chestnut mare.

Caius experienced a frisson of disquiet when Kaeto's incisive gaze flickered over the new master of hounds. Decian had just arrived with Pip. Both were mounted on common roan ponies, with the hunting pack milling excitedly around them. But there was surely nothing for Kaeto to latch onto. At worst, he might make note of the fact that the emperor's new houndsman shared the same rich skin tone that he could have glimpsed on the bound hands of one of the nameless bastard half-brothers he'd ordered to their deaths over the past few weeks. That was all... and it was nothing. There were countless men of foreign birth or bloodline living in Amarius.

As the sun crested the palace walls, illuminating the courtyard by the main gates, they awaited only the emperor himself. Caius' gray gelding pawed the cobbles restlessly, eager for the chase. The dogs clustered around their two handlers, many of the beasts gazing up at Decian adoringly. He hoped that expression of canine loyalty boded well for the next few hours. It would be maddening to come so close to success in his self-appointed task of getting Decian away safely, only to have everything collapse around them in the last few moments.

Finally, the approach of many hooves heralded the arrival of Constanzus and his retinue of guards. Aelio rode at the emperor's right hand, sitting astride his bay courser. Another five soldiers flanked Constanzus' white stallion, silent sentry against any who might wish him harm.

The emperor had grown gaunt in recent months, as whatever illness or curse had befallen him took its toll on his body as well as his mind. Nonetheless, he sat straight in the saddle, the prospect of the hunt bringing a light to his eye that little else could manage these days.

"Everything is prepared?" he called to the assembled group, his voice a pale echo of the battlefield roar that had once commanded legions. "Then let us depart!"

On his command, horses and hounds headed for the gates and the open land beyond the edges of the city. The company was a large one, consisting of not only the hunters and dogs, but also an entourage of servants and wagons carrying the pavilions that would be set up for refreshments. Additionally, there were the palace guards commanded by Aelio, numbering perhaps two dozen, who would follow them on the hunt with eyes for the royal family's security, rather than the quarry.

Amarian citizens in the streets stopped what they were doing and moved aside for the small army of horses, hounds, and wagons. Most of them bowed deeply, avoiding eye contact. However, Caius' neck prickled as he noted the way that a few looked up from their obeisance with hard, angry expressions. He caught Aelio's gaze for a moment, seeing the same awareness reflected back at him in the palace commander's eyes.

Unrest was growing within the city, coiling in the shadows like an angry serpent hiding under a log. Still, no one was foolish enough to attempt any overt action against the large, well-armed royal party. When the tension inevitably erupted into the open, Caius suspected the city would tear at its own flanks long before aiming its venomous strike directly for the head.

They rode through the outskirts of the capital. Buildings gave way to fields, and eventually to pristine forest unspoiled by human habitation. The air grew sweeter as they left the stench of the city behind. The Silver Wood was royal land, set aside for the emperor's pleasure. Poaching within its boundaries was grounds for having an eye put out or a hand removed. Repeat offenders were executed.

As a result, the place was teeming with wildlife of every description. Deer and hare were thick in its dappled depths. Many a farmer cursed the woods as a breeding ground for wolves, boar, and foxes that roamed abroad, damaging cropland and killing livestock in their smallholdings.

The hounds wrestled each other and yipped excitedly as they entered the forest, eager to explore the myriad of scents drifting on the breeze. The pack moved like a stream of choppy water around Decian and Pip's stocky mounts, little waves of excitement cresting here and there. Caius could not help noticing how utterly ill at ease Decian appeared on horseback, bouncing stiffly in the saddle with the reins held awkwardly high.

He winced at the younger man's lack of skill, and chastised himself for it a moment later. What did he expect, for god's sake? It was almost as if Decian had been raised as a commoner and then stuck in prison for the last who-knew-how-many years, rather than learning to ride and hunt like the son of nobility he was.

With luck, his lack of experience on horseback wouldn't matter. The master of hounds controlled the hunting pack with the curled horn hanging from his saddle. No doubt Pip had spent the last two days tutoring Decian in the various signals and commands. He wouldn't need to keep pace with the dogs at all times.

It would be fine, surely. At this point, all Caius could do was hope.

They ventured deeper into the woods, the dense stand of trees cut through with meticulously maintained trails and paths. The dogs sniffed eagerly along the edges of the smooth track along which they were riding, but did not scatter into the forest. Before long, the group passed into a large clearing where the pavilions would be erected. The wagons came to a halt, servants immediately swarming over them to unload and ready things for the royal party's comfort. Aelio spoke to his men, going over final plans for the coming hunt, while Caius forced himself to stay out of the tribuni's way.

He was no longer a soldier in the same sense as Aelio and his underlings. His fighting career had ended four years ago on the western border, with the wet thud of a barbarian battleaxe embedding itself in his flesh. He stood back and let the palace commander do his job, instead watching surreptitiously as Decian and Pip disappeared into the maze of trails with the dogs, seeking a covert where game worth hunting might be flushed out.

Caius turned at the approach of another horse, surprised to find Bruccias sidling his mare within conversational range. Constanzus' youngest son was a dark-haired, well-favored youth of nineteen who'd inherited something of his father's square shoulders and stubborn jaw line. He was also as oily as a mink, adept at greasing the wheels of power whenever he thought that doing so might somehow benefit him.

"A pleasant day for a hunt," said the young princep, as though he and Caius were old drinking friends engaging in casual conversation.

Caius wondered what Bruccius sought to gain from him today. It didn't even occur to him that the friendly gambit might be genuine.

"His Imperial Majesty has always had an excellent eye for the chase," he replied, noncommittal. "It's good that your elder brother was able to join us this morning."

Bruccias laughed lightly, as though at an inside joke. "Oh, indeed." He cleared his throat, and Caius thought, *now we come to it.* "Jesting aside, I must admit, I've been wondering what you make of my brother's recent... *crusade*, Legatus."

There was absolutely no reason for the question to make Caius' heart beat faster, or make prickles of sweat break out across the nape of his neck.

"Proclus has undertaken a crusade?" he asked, being deliberately obtuse. "I can't say I'd noticed, Princep."

Bruccias stared at him unblinkingly. Had Caius been either younger or less jaded than he was, he might have found that flat gaze disconcerting.

"Playing the fool doesn't suit you, Caius," Bruccias said shrewdly. "It's clear you disapprove of Kaeto's private war against our father's bastards. Proclus disapproves as well. So do I. We thought you should know that."

Privately, Caius doubted whether Proclus had even *noticed* the steady stream of young men entering the palace gates over the past weeks, never to leave again. He also wasn't certain what, exactly, Bruccias was getting at.

He summoned a suitably noncommittal reply. "Prisoners in the empire serve their sentence at His Imperial Majesty's pleasure. My opinion on the disposition of that sentence carries no weight."

Still, Bruccias continued to watch him with unnerving intensity. "His Imperial Majesty's pleasure had nothing to do with it, Legatus—as I suspect you well know. Kaeto has been taking liberties."

Caius wished mightily for a convenient exit from the conversation. "I wouldn't presume to comment on matters of which I know nothing, Princep," was all he said.

Finally, Bruccias blinked. "Of course not. I only wish to know whether Proclus can count on your support, should our dear brother attempt to reach even higher for things beyond his grasp."

So that was it. Bruccias was feeling out the sentiment of the inner court… not anything more sinister that that. Nothing relating to Caius' recent actions in saving Decian, as his paranoia had tried to suggest.

"I serve the rightful succession," Caius replied gruffly, wondering if that was truly the case anymore. Soldiers who served the empire loyally tended not to disobey the direct orders of the second in line to the throne.

"As you have done for far longer than I've been alive," Bruccias said with oily graciousness.

"Forgive me, Legatus, for implying it could be otherwise."

Caius was reminded, not for the first time, of the many reasons he so disliked the emperor's youngest son. It was a great pity that he also disliked the emperor's *other* sons—though for different reasons. Thankfully, he was saved from having to come up with a diplomatic reply by the sound of a hunting horn echoing through the trees.

"Ah!" Bruccias cried, a smile lighting up his handsome face. "It seems the chase is on! Come, Caius—let us see what the dogs have scared up for us."

The young princep wheeled his mare and galloped off, while Caius followed at a more sedate pace, reining in his eager mount. His gelding would happily have charged ahead at full speed, but Caius was well aware that he was included in hunts such as this only as a courtesy these days. He carried no weapon except the ceremonial sword and dagger at his belt—neither of which was a generally preferred method for dispatching game.

Since his injury, he could no longer fire a crossbow or hurl a spear reliably while also controlling a horse. And while some soldiers might revel in hurtling after a deer over ditches and logs, risking a fall or a mount's broken leg for the sake of meat that could be more easily acquired elsewhere—Caius was not one of them. He headed toward the sound of the horn at a sedate canter, the gray horse champing impatiently at the bit.

Members of the hunt tended to sort themselves into two groups fairly quickly—those for whom the chance to make the kill represented glory and increased status, and those who either felt that they had to make an appearance, or who genuinely enjoyed a morning's canter through a forest with the occasional stream to splash through or fallen tree to leap.

On his best days, Caius might count himself among the latter group. The Silver Wood was undeniably a beautiful place, and having the wind in one's face and a good horse between one's legs for an hour or three was not an unpleasant proposition. Unfortunately, today was not destined to be numbered amongst Caius' best days.

Or... perhaps it should be, given that he had finally made some small stand against the many injustices surrounding him. Whatever the case, Caius' main concern on this particular hunt was ensuring that Decian got away cleanly. He was confident that once away from Amarius, the young man would be good to his word, disappearing never to be heard from again.

Lucky man, he caught himself thinking.

Riding near the front of the less ambitious group of hunters, Caius registered a downed tree ahead, its trunk lodged across the trail at an angle. He steadied his gelding and approached the lower side, shifting his weight forward and giving the animal its head as powerful muscles bunched beneath him, launching them over the obstacle.

He absorbed the impact of the landing with his knees—something else that had been considerably easier a few years ago. Several other riders followed his lead, but then he heard a commotion behind him indicating that someone's horse had balked, or otherwise caused a problem.

Caius didn't look back, since it wasn't his job to babysit soft courtiers who couldn't properly sit a horse over a low jump. Unbidden, his thoughts flashed to Decian, bouncing in the saddle with the reins held stiffly in front of him. Thankfully, Decian struck him as a man with enough sense to ride around any obstacles he wasn't confident of mastering on horseback.

Ahead, more hunting horns sounded, indicating the quarry was in sight.

"What do you think they've got?" puffed a pale courtier riding at Caius' right flank.

"Does it really matter?" Caius replied.

Suddenly unwilling to pretend enthusiasm for this hunt that should never have happened in the first place, he allowed his eager horse to stretch into a gallop that left his companions behind. The animal leapt across the next ditch almost gleefully, its breath coming in rhythmic snorts.

Ahead, he could hear the excited cries of the hunters, and he gathered that the lead riders had caught up to whatever prey the dogs had flushed from cover. In the confusion of trees and crisscrossing animal trails, it took some time to find the main party. By the time he finally did, the day's excitement appeared to be over. Caius could make out no details across the length of the clearing where the final confrontation had taken place — only the dogs milling around whatever creature had been brought down, while Pip and Decian on their fat ponies waded into the midst of the pack to call them off the carcass.

The emperor's white horse trotted toward him, and Caius straightened to unthinking attention in the saddle.

"Your Imperial Majesty," he greeted.

"Ah, Caius!" The emperor's eyes shone with an almost fanatical light from within his gaunt face. "A good hunt! Kaeto and Bruccias brought down the beast together—though I think it was Kaeto's spear that pierced its heart."

"I'm pleased to hear it," Caius managed.

Constanzus waved an airy hand. "Yes, yes. Well, do carry on, Legatus."

Already, the emperor's customary distracted expression was reasserting itself. Caius felt the increasingly familiar sense of a heavy weight clenching cold and clammy inside his gut. The leader of an empire that spanned continents was failing before his eyes, and no one worthy of the title stood waiting in the wings to replace him.

He swallowed hard. "Yes, Your Majesty." But Constanzus had already wandered off.

Across the glen, the dogs had clustered around Pip, who led them away from the kill with a shrill whistle and a snap of his whip. Decian trotted toward Caius, and a new, much more pleasant kind of tension coiled in his chest. The younger man smiled at him with a sort of wary hopefulness as he approached. Something about that smile made Caius' throat ache.

"Greetings, Legatus," Decian said with a sense of formality that didn't quite ring true. "It looks as

60

though I'm missing two dogs. I figured I'd send the rest of the pack back with Pip while I nip off and look for them. I assume you'll let the others know, in case anyone wonders where I've disappeared to?"

The wink that accompanied the words was so quick Caius almost missed it.

"As long as you think you can manage it without falling off that pony," he returned.

That startled a huffed breath of laughter from Decian. "I won't lie—my arse may never recover from the last couple of hours," he said. Then his tone softened into something more genuine. "Thank you for everything you've done."

Caius made a concerted attempt to ground himself in this moment—appreciating the fact that he'd helped an innocent man to freedom, while ignoring the impulse to stare too long at the aforementioned man's square, hard-muscled shoulders and slender waist.

"Call me Caius," he replied. "I'll pass on the message to anyone who asks. Good hunting, Decian."

"Good hunting… *Caius*." Decian smiled his crooked little half-smile again, before reining the pony around with exaggerated, unpracticed movements. Caius watched him go, finding himself oddly surprised by the anticlimactic nature of it all.

SEVEN

After ensuring that Decian was safely away, Caius rejoined the main party and dismounted, handing his horse off to a servant so he could stretch his legs for a bit and try to unknot the cramped and twisted muscles in his bad shoulder. Unfortunately, this tactical decision had the unintended consequence of exposing his metaphorical flank to a bevy of over-excited young whelps who thought a beast hounded to its death in the forest was somehow worthy of awe.

"It's magnificent, is it not?" crowed one. "Quite the largest I've ever seen."

"You *must* come and see before the butchers start hacking at it!" exclaimed another.

And so it was that Caius found himself being chivvied along to look at a dead animal lying in the grass at the edge of a glen. He let the inane chattering of the courtiers wash over him — wishing only for the peace and privacy of his quarters, now that Decian was gone and the thing was finally done.

The little knot of men approached the site of the kill, and the courtier on Caius' right said, "Look at those antlers! They must be six feet across, at least!"

Caius' feet brought him to an abrupt halt at the edge of the circle of trampled grass. Blood coated the broken stalks, and his vision swam for a moment as the image before him blurred double with the image from his dream.

From his *memory*.

A great stag lay in the bloodied grass, its hide smeared with crimson. Spears jutted from its ribs and flank. Its dark eyes stared through Caius, and its tongue jutted obscenely from its mouth, swollen and purple. For a moment, the play of shadows from the overhanging branches darkened its antler-tips, making them appear shiny with gore to his addled gaze.

He took a single, involuntary step back before catching himself and blinking rapidly.

No.

This was not the otherworldly abomination that had killed his father when he was a boy of eight. There were only two spears, not three—hurled by the hands of Kaeto and Bruccias. The stag's antlers were not blood-soaked; it was merely a trick of shadow and light. Its eyes did not glow as they had in his dream.

He glanced around furtively, his breath coming fast and shallow. No one had noticed his lapse. They were all too busy fawning over the supposed greatness of the two princes who had ridden down an exhausted hart and killed it, as though the feat had been some enviable battlefield victory.

"Is it not a majestic creature?" sighed the man who had waxed poetical earlier about the stag's antlers. He glanced at Caius, clearly expecting a response.

It probably was, but it's not anymore, Caius thought.

"I need a piss," he said aloud, aware that his voice emerged hoarse. Before anyone could express outrage at his lack of appreciation for the carcass bleeding onto the dirt, he turned and escaped into the trees — ostensibly to find some privacy so he could relieve himself.

His heart still thundered painfully against his chest. He kept walking until the sounds of the hunting party faded to a distant buzz behind him, and fetched up against the sturdy bole of an ancient oak tree.

It was ridiculous. He'd seen dead stags before, many times. Hell, he'd taken a few himself in his younger days. If it hadn't been for that *fucking* dream last night...

Caius growled in frustration at his unruly mind, fumbling with the laces of his breeches and smallclothes — as though following through with his feeble excuse for fleeing the glade would somehow erase the lapse that had preceded it. He stepped back and aimed a weak stream of piss at the base of the tree, silently cursing himself, his nightmare, the failing emperor who thought this hunt had been a good idea, and stags who were too stupid to escape a pack of baying hounds.

A twig snapped somewhere off to his left, and he turned his head sharply toward the noise.

It might have been another member of the hunting party come to relieve his bladder. It might have been an animal. But the fine hair at the back of Caius' neck prickled unpleasantly, and he tucked himself away as quickly as he could without making it look like he'd noticed something amiss. He turned casually in the direction of the sound, his right hand resting on the hilt of his dagger.

A breath of air caressed his cheek as a crossbow bolt flew past and embedded itself in the tree with a sharp *thunk*, two inches from his temple.

In an instant, the heady awareness of imminent death sang through his veins, dispelling his earlier disquiet between one heartbeat and the next. Caius was already in motion, putting the tree trunk between himself and the archer's position. His thoughts flew — was this an attack on the royal family? Or had he merely stumbled upon a poacher desperate enough to add murder to his crimes if it meant silencing a witness who might drag him before the imperial magistrate?

A second arrow sliced through the loose sleeve of his linen shirt, drawing a burning line across his left bicep before burying itself in wood. He cursed and ripped it free, darting sideways into the trees. That one had come from a completely different direction.

This was no poacher.

He could cry out for help — attempt to shout a warning — but he'd purposely wandered far away from the main party. It would take them some time to find him, especially now that he was on the move. It was also unlikely that he'd be able to convey the nature of the threat effectively enough to keep any responders from stumbling into a hail of arrows.

How many assailants were there? *Damnation*. If there were any possibility of this being an organized, large-scale attack, there was nothing else for it.

"*Ambush!*" he roared in his best battlefield bellow — rusty now, after four years of palace life. "*Guards!* Protect the royals!"

Caius ducked and dodged through the trees, not following any established path or trail. If he could take down one of the two currently hunting him, he could make his way back to the clearing with less chance of being cut down for his troubles.

Another crossbow bolt whizzed past, going wide in the confusion of tree trunks and brush. He tracked its direction and altered course, heading for the source of the shot. Distantly, he could just make out the sound of shouting as the hunting party and its guards reacted to his cry of warning.

Closer, the sound of a would-be assassin on the move held his attention firmly on his goal. It was impossible to move silently in this tangle of branches and underbrush, with piles of fallen leaves crunching underfoot. With luck, their surroundings would also negate much of the advantage his opponents held with their ranged weapons. Unfortunately, the forest was also a poor venue for sword fighting. Though naturally left-handed, Caius had made a point over the past four years of becoming competent as a right-handed swordsman. Now, though, his dagger was the best option in his limited arsenal.

He just had to get close enough to use it without getting skewered by a crossbow bolt first.

The assailant he was tracking changed course, cutting toward him at an angle that made Caius think he was attempting to get in front of him for an ambush. He increased his pace through the vines and thickets, his lungs burning from the unaccustomed exertion. Indeed, moments later he stumbled without warning into a small clearing. The bare patch in the woods had been obscured from view until he was practically upon it.

The archer stood at the far end, dressed in dark clothing, with a mask obscuring the lower half of his face. Perhaps a dozen strides separated them. The man whirled to face him, lifting a loaded double-bolt crossbow into position in the same motion.

Instinct had Caius flipping the dagger in his right hand to grasp the blade between thumb and forefinger, before letting it fly in an overhand throw. The reality of being both out of practice and naturally left-handed meant that the blade embedded itself in the meat of the man's arm rather than anyplace more vital.

The assassin cried out, the crossbow releasing one of its twin bolts with a twang as it slipped from his injured grasp. The bolt missed Caius by a hand's breadth, flying over his head to crash into the brush. Caius unsheathed his sword with a snarl and charged. The assassin drew a blade with his good hand, steel meeting steel as they clashed. Caius hacked at his opponent with the vicious recklessness that had earned him his reputation on the battlefield over the course of a military career spanning decades.

It didn't matter that he was well into his forty-sixth year, or that he'd not seen a battle since the one that had ruined his shoulder. It didn't matter that his left arm was largely useless for swordplay after the injury. His opponent, injured and outclassed, stood no chance fighting him blade against blade. Caius hacked and slashed, knocking the other man's sword to the side and kneeing him in the stomach.

The man stumbled back, his shoulders impacting a tree at the edge of the clearing. A moment later, he looked down in confusion at the slice that opened his gut. Caius watched the man's sword hilt slide from nerveless fingers. His hands came up to cradle the ruin of his stomach, uselessly. A moment later, he slid down the rough bark of the tree trunk to sprawl on the ground, groaning as he bled out.

Caius sheathed his sword. He moved cautiously, leaning down to retrieve the discarded crossbow, still with its single remaining bolt loaded and cocked. A rustle came from the underbrush to his right. When he straightened and whipped around, it was to find the second assassin aiming his own crossbow at Caius' heart.

68

EIGHT

Caius wouldn't have voluntarily chosen to engage in a duel of crossbows where he was forced to fire right-handed. His finger tightened on the trigger at the same instant as the assassin's. The twangs of two bolts releasing reached his ears simultaneously.

He grunted as nauseating pain flared in his left thigh, the impact spinning him to the side. His attacker slumped forward, free hand curling around the bolt bristling from his ribcage as he fell to the ground and started jerking. Caius tried to catch himself against the nearest tree trunk with his left hand, but missed, his scarred shoulder hitting it instead. The twisted muscles screamed, a throbbing counterpoint to the fiery burn of the arrow embedded in his leg.

His jaw ached with the force of his gritted teeth as he steadied himself, knowing he needed to stay alert and on his feet in the event of more archers hiding in the woods. A quick glance at the body near his feet confirmed that the first assassin had a quiver of crossbow bolts slung over his shoulder, but Caius feared that leaning down and trying to grab one so he could reload his stolen weapon might make him pass out. Before he could convince himself to attempt it anyway, the shouts of approaching guards and hunters responding to his raised alarm reached his ears.

"Here!" he cried hoarsely. "Look sharp—there might be archers in the trees!"

Aelio appeared first, sword drawn and blue eyes snapping fire. Then, to Caius' distant surprise, Decian charged into the clearing from the opposite direction, skidding to a halt as he took in the carnage and the arrow sticking out of Caius' leg. With the immediate crisis apparently over, Caius let the growing heaviness in his body drag him down in a semi-controlled collapse against the base of the tree, hissing a bit as the wound in his leg protested.

"The emperor?" he asked, directing the question to Aelio.

"Safe and well guarded," said the tribuni. "What happened here, Legatus?"

Caius raised a shaking hand to scrub at his face. "I went for a piss, and nearly took an arrow through the skull for my trouble. There were two of them… as you can see."

Decian seemed to wrench himself free of his paralysis. "You're hurt," he said, giving the downed assassin next to Caius a wide berth as he approached.

"It's not serious," Caius said, giving his leg a long look and sighing.

"There's an arrow sticking out of you," Decian replied rather pointedly.

Aelio snorted. "Definitely not for the first time, houndsman. Though, one might hope it will be the last. No offense, Caius, but you're supposed to be retired from active duty."

"Tell that to the random assassins roaming the woods," he grumbled.

Aelio shook his head and gestured at the arrow. "You want to take that out now? Or wait until you're back at the palace?"

Caius made a disgruntled noise and grasped the shaft right handed, yanking it free in a single, sharp movement. Decian flinched. Blood welled from the wound, but didn't spurt—as he'd known it wouldn't. He tossed the bolt aside and untied the decorative blue sash from his waist.

"It went in at an angle," he told Decian, who was looking decidedly pale beneath his tawny skin—especially for someone who'd barely batted an eye while a man was being torn apart by dogs a handful of days ago. "Don't worry, it mostly lodged under the skin rather than in the muscle. Someone help me bind it and give me a shoulder to lean on. Where's my horse?"

"Back at the clearing with the kill, I should imagine," Aelio said, as Decian hesitantly leant a hand to wrap the blue cloth around the wound and tie it tight. More people were arriving, and Caius cursed silently as he truly registered for the first time that Decian hadn't made it away as planned.

Aelio prodded the second assailant's body with the toe of his boot, looking down with a frown. "Next question—who were they, and what were they after?" He leaned down and tugged off the man's mask, revealing nondescript Alyrion features.

Leg bandaged — after a fashion, at least — Caius accepted Decian's hand up, steadying himself between the younger man and the tree at his back until his lightheadedness subsided.

"Not poachers, that's for sure," he gritted, carefully testing a bit of weight on the leg. It held, notwithstanding the stab of pain radiating outward from the wound. "Assassins after the emperor and his sons, probably. I must have surprised them as they were trying to sneak up on the main party."

Aelio's expression hardened. "In which case, we have an even bigger problem with security than we originally thought. It's not as though this hunting expedition was advertised to the public."

"As you say," Caius agreed. His wound flared as he took another step, still leaning on Decian. "*Fuck*, I should've killed the bastards slower. And a *lot* more painfully."

Aelio raised a wry eyebrow. "If it meant we could have questioned them before they died, I can't disagree."

"I can't believe you two are joking about this," Decian muttered.

Caius shot him a sideways glance, suddenly struck by the warm line of Decian's body pressed against his. He cleared his throat and looked away.

"Didn't you have some missing dogs to look for?" he prodded.

"They can wait for a bit," Decian replied grimly.

"Come, Legatus. Let's get you back to the others," Aelio said, before turning to the additional men who'd arrived. "Search the area. Make sure no one else is skulking around. Watch your backs." With that, the tribuni sheathed his sword. He and Decian maneuvered Caius between them, working around his bad shoulder as best they could.

"Your arm's bleeding, too," Decian pointed out, frowning at the line of red soaking Caius' left shirtsleeve.

"It's just a graze," he said, having forgotten all about it in the face of subsequent events.

"If you say so." Decian's tone was skeptical.

They hobbled through the underbrush, cursing as it dragged at them, until they reached a trail. Caius was pretty thoroughly turned around by that point, but Aelio seemed to know where he was going. Eventually, they did, in fact, reach the clearing with its bloody, trampled circle of grass at one edge. The butchers had continued their work despite the excitement, and the creature from Caius' bad dreams was now little more than a stack of meat and a pair of trophy antlers.

He still had to look away from it.

In the shade of the trees beyond, the members of the royal family were gathered together on horseback, surrounded on all sides by a tight pack of guards bristling with weapons. Caius ran his eyes over the four figures at the center of the circle out of habit, ensuring that they were all unhurt and accounted for.

"There were two assassins armed with blades and crossbows in the woods, Your Majesties," Aelio reported once they were close enough to be heard. "The legatus killed them, but was injured during the fight. I have other men searching the forest to make certain no others are hiding there, but we should return to the palace immediately for Your Majesties' safety."

Proclus ran bloodshot eyes over their sad little procession. "Old Caius killed them, eh?" He laughed, short and harsh. "Still a bit of life in the one-armed soldier after all, then. Who'd've thought?"

Irritation at the casual slight would have been unseemly. It also required more energy than Caius really possessed at the moment. Any ruffled feathers he might have suffered were quickly soothed by the way Constanzus looked at him, dark brows furrowing—clearly seeing him properly.

"Well done, Legatus," he said, sounding more like the man Caius had known, and less like the pale shadow he'd become. "Once again, you bleed to protect us."

"It is my duty, Your Imperial Majesty," he managed, taken aback by the degree to which such praise could still affect him. "Nothing more."

He wasn't oblivious to the fact of Decian supporting his right side, face to face with the father he didn't know and the half-brother who would prefer to see him dead. Kaeto sniffed, oblivious to the identity of his escaped victim standing mere yards away.

"Perhaps the legatus should retire for medical attention and rest after such unexpected exertion," the princep suggested, as though he had an ounce of care for anyone but himself.

"You're quite correct, Your Majesty," Aelio agreed quickly. His gaze flicked between Caius and the royal family uncertainly. "I could—"

"You are needed here," Proclus interrupted. "If there is danger to us, your place is guarding us during our return to the palace."

"I'll take care of him," Decian said immediately.

Caius grimaced. "The missing dogs…"

"*Will be fine*," Decian finished for him. "Pip can deal with them."

Kaeto looked down his nose from his elevated position on horseback. "And who is this?"

A chill ran down Caius' spine that had nothing to do with exertion or blood loss.

"He's the new—" Aelio began.

"No one of import, Your Majesty," Caius interrupted, speaking over him. "I will allow him to help me back to my quarters, and no doubt be recovered enough to return to duty in a few days."

"Yes, yes," said the emperor, waving an airy hand. "Do go on. You're suddenly looking rather pale, Legatus."

Caius bowed as best he could, elbowing Decian when he didn't immediately follow suit. As quickly as was feasible, he dragged Decian away as though he were the one with two good legs and Decian, the injured one. Subtle, it probably wasn't, based on the look Aelio gave him as they left.

"So, was that…?" Decian started to ask.

"The Emperor of Alyrios and his three sons, yes," Caius muttered.

"Huh," Decian said. "Which one was the asshole who ordered me executed? I recognized his voice."

Caius pressed his lips together, and not only because his damned leg hurt. "That would be Princep Kaeto. The middle son."

Decian didn't reply.

It took a few minutes to track down someone who could retrieve Caius' horse. The gray gelding snorted mistrustfully at Decian, who eyed him with equal distaste.

"Your horse is very… big," he observed.

"Yes. Still, you'll forgive me if I prefer not to ride your pony back to the city," Caius sniped, aware that his tone sounded more than a little peevish.

Decian shrugged. "As you like. You're the one who has to figure out how to get into the saddle."

Caius looked at the tall gelding, and sighed.

NINE

The less said about the logistics of Caius getting mounted, the better. In the end, it required three men, a tree stump, and quite a bit of creative cursing. Meanwhile, a guard had retrieved the roan pony from the forest where Decian had abandoned it during the excitement. When they were ready to depart, however, Decian decreed firmly that he would walk back rather than riding.

Aelio's men had found no trace of anyone else hiding in the woods. Caius and Decian left ahead of the main party, since it would take time to pack up the wagons and organize the men for the return to the palace. Once Caius was confident they were well out of hearing range of the others, he turned a frown toward the younger man walking even with his horse's shoulder.

"You could still leave, you know," he said in a low tone.

Decian glanced up at him, eyes dark and guarded. "I heard you shouting about an ambush, back in the forest. Figured I owed you one after the kennels." He shrugged. "There'll be other hunts. And anyway, the guards are already getting to know me. It's not like this was my only chance to get away."

Caius swallowed another protest—knowing the other man was right, but still taken aback by the jolt of worry he'd felt when Kaeto had expressed casual interest in Decian's identity.

Decian raised an eyebrow. "So, are we going to look for a surgeon when we get back? Is there one in the palace? There must be, right?"

Caius felt his features twist with distaste. "Might as well have asked the butchers in the hunting party to have a go at me once they were done with the stag. The wound just needs cleaning and bandaging, that's all."

Decian glanced up at him with a raised eyebrow. "If you say so. Does this kind of thing happen to you often, then?"

Caius snorted. "I was a soldier for nearly three decades. The job comes with its share of wounds."

"Like your shoulder?" prompted Decian, who could hardly have failed to notice the defect during the awkward three-man shuffle back to the clearing earlier.

"Yes. I took a blow from a battle axe four years ago," he said. "Can't say I really recommend it."

Decian nodded. "I don't blame you. I managed to get through ten years of prison with only a single flogging and the occasional beating by the guards. Can't say I recommend any of it, to be honest."

Caius remembered the mess of scar tissue he'd seen on Decian's bare back in the kennels.

"What was the flogging for?" he asked.

"I helped another prisoner escape," Decian said.

Caius blinked at him. Alyrion prisons weren't exactly known for their leniency. "Surprised it wasn't more than a flogging, for something like that."

Bitterness crept into Decian's tone. "Being a nobleman's bastard comes with a few benefits, apparently. Right up until the day when it doesn't anymore."

Caius digested that for a few moments.

"What about the man you helped?" he asked eventually. "Did he make it out?"

"I'm not sure," Decian replied. "They didn't tell me. I never saw a body, so he might've done. Of course, I was also delirious with fever and blood loss for more than a week after the whipping, so I could have missed it. I hope he did get away. He was nice, and he had other people who cared about him enough to try to sneak in and smuggle him out."

Caius wasn't prepared for the sharp ache those words engendered. How long had it been since he'd had people in his life who'd cared for him that much?

Unbidden, Serah's face appeared in his memory—his sweet wife, rosy-cheeked, with long, brown hair and twinkling gray eyes. They'd both been so young when she'd died... matched in an arranged marriage that had hardly lasted long enough to blossom into more. Yet her loss had hollowed him out as nothing else ever had. Diminished him in ways he couldn't fully express, not even all these years later.

In the army, he'd had comrades, of course— men as close as brothers. He'd known the intimacy of trusting that the man next to you would lay down his life for yours, as you would do for him in turn. Sometimes, there had been intimacy of other kinds among the men, as well—in a setting where such liaisons were quietly overlooked since they helped with morale.

Too many of Caius' fellow soldiers had fallen at his side during battle. Too many had fallen while under his command. Eventually, he'd fallen in battle as well, in the course of protecting his emperor... and now he was alone in a world that didn't suit his talents, surrounded by people to whom he was either a useless relic or an embarrassing hindrance.

"Whether he made it out alive or not, your friend was still a lucky man to have such friends," he managed.

They continued in silence. Caius directed his horse down smaller side streets as they reentered the city, rather than staying on the main vaia with its milling crowds shooting them furtive, angry glances. Eventually, they arrived at the outer wall of the imperial quarter, where Caius made a point of introducing Decian to the pair of guards manning the east gate.

One of the men took a single glance at Caius' leg and asked if he wanted to send for the physician, but Caius waved him off with a growled negative. "Send a stableboy to meet us at my quarters and take my horse, though," he added grudgingly.

Passing through the gate, they continued into the maze of walls and buildings. The dwelling belonging to Caius was part of a larger block of tightly packed *insulae* located on the western side of the palace compound, housing courtiers and other advisors to the royal family. After half a lifetime spent bunking in various forts and encampments, Caius had always considered the house to be ridiculously grand with its atrium and colonnaded garden... but at least it was private. After his years of eschewing social contact, few people bothered him here. Even the middle-aged slave woman who cooked and cleaned for him knew enough to perform most of her work while he was out.

A fresh-faced stable lad jogged up while he was maneuvering himself out of the saddle — a process thankfully simpler than getting into it had been. Caius tossed the boy a copper coin as he led the gelding away, and accepted Decian's support to hobble inside.

Unnecessarily grand or not, Caius still felt a bit of tension unwind from his shoulders as he entered the familiar haven. It felt decidedly odd to welcome another person inside the house. Decian looked around with something uncomfortably close to awe. Caius directed him through the atrium with its burbling marble fountain, past the hallway with the kitchen on one side and his office on the other, and into the open garden surrounded by white columns.

His bedroom — along with three identical guest rooms that he never used — opened onto the airy space. Inside, wood and kindling lay ready in the grate, placed there by Tertia, the housekeeper, in anticipation of his return.

"How many people live in this place?" Decian asked, still taking everything in as though his neck was on a swivel-joint. "It's like a palace within a palace."

"Just me," Caius said gruffly, peeling himself away from Decian's support and limping across the room to his bed. He unbuckled his swordbelt and laid it on the table before sinking onto the edge of the mattress, his bad leg stretched out in front of him, heel resting on the floor. Once there, he realized that his ambition to care for his injuries had evaporated at some point during the journey. Left to his own devices, at this moment he would have done nothing more useful than collapse onto the feather mattress and sleep.

"Just you? *Seriously*?" Decian echoed. "Being a legatus clearly comes with a few more perks than being a nobleman's bastard, even on a good day."

"It's not so much being a legatus," Caius said, "as being someone who stood between the emperor and a barbarian's axe on the battlefield. That part does come with a few benefits, it's true."

Decian ran a weather eye up and down Caius' body. "You're about to keel over, aren't you," he observed, not really phrasing it as a question. "Get your shirt off so I can see that graze on your arm. Then we'll tackle the rest."

Unused to being fussed over, Caius felt his mind settle into relieved compliance despite his best intentions. He opened the row of hook-and-eye closures securing his leather jerkin and slid it off—right arm first, then the left. Next, he pulled the hem of his linen shirt free from his trousers and shrugged out of it, dipping his head to ease himself free of the wide collar without the requirement of raising his bad arm very far. The blood-stiffened linen had become glued to his skin as it dried. He winced as he pulled it away from the shallow wound where the second arrow had carved a furrow in his bicep.

Decian leaned close, grasping him above the elbow and gently turning his upper arm toward the light from the window. The fine hairs all over Caius' body stood up in response to the touch, and he cleared his throat to distract himself.

"There's a bottle half full of brandy on the shelf," he said in a tone that was purposely gruff. "Get it for me, please."

Decian gave him a wry look, his face somehow both too close and not close enough to Caius'. "Are you planning on drinking it or using it to clean the wounds?" he asked.

"Both," Caius replied without hesitation.

The huff of amusement he got in response did nothing to quiet his rattling thoughts, but at least Decian did as he'd asked. Left to his own devices for a few moments, he craned around to look, confirming that the slice in his skin wasn't ragged enough to require debridement. It was oozing again after he'd pulled the sleeve free of the clotting blood, but it would probably do better without a bandage, even so.

Decian returned and handed him the uncorked brandy bottle before gesturing at the wound. "You should leave that open to the air, assuming you can keep it clean. It'll scab in a few hours," he said, echoing Caius' thoughts.

"Agreed." Caius tipped the bottle to his lips right-handed, swallowing without decorum. The brandy burned going down, but it would take a lot more than what he had available to truly dull the pain of the next few minutes.

"Do you have anything here to bandage your leg?" Decian asked. "Anything *clean*, that is to say."

"There should be towels in the kitchen somewhere," he said. "You can use a couple of those."

Once Decian left to look for the linen, Caius gritted his teeth and sloshed a bit of the brandy over the graze on his arm. Pain flared, which was at least a momentary distraction from the insistent throbbing in his damned leg. He breathed through it, using his discarded shirt to mop at the rivulets of reddish brown spidering down his arm before they could drip onto the bedding.

By the time Decian returned with a bowl of clean water and the linen, Caius was fumbling at the tight knot of makeshift bandaging over the hole in his thigh with fingers that didn't want to cooperate. Decian batted his hands away. "Let me. Get your breeches unlaced."

Between them, they got him stripped down to his smallclothes, which had mostly escaped harm except for a bit of blood staining the bottom edge.

"Lie down," Decian ordered, pushing Caius onto his back and helping him lift his injured leg onto the bed. He perched on the edge of the mattress to examine the ragged hole. Caius draped his right arm across his eyes, wishing once more that he could just sleep for the rest of the day and deal with the wound later.

All thoughts of sleep fled in an instant when a callused hand closed on his thigh, resting a few inches below the wound. The touch was utterly innocent — a way to steady the leg as Decian prepared to clean up the injury so he could see it properly. Innocent intentions or not, the blood rushed urgently to Caius' prick, which twitched hard against his smalls, tenting the loose material.

Cursing his body's longstanding tendency to blur the lines between fighting and fucking — not to mention the effects of the brandy on his self-control — Caius let his arm slide away from his eyes so he could judge Decian's expression. Caius was both too old and too experienced to succumb to irrational panic over another man's reaction to his sexual proclivities… which wasn't to say that such reactions couldn't turn ugly, given Alyrion social mores. He didn't fear Decian. The man was unarmed, and in no position to make trouble for himself. Even so, Caius wasn't ignorant of his own vulnerability given the current situation.

Decian looked from Caius' cock to his face, his pleasant features tinged with wry surprise. "Well, well. So, there's a human being lurking beneath that gruff exterior after all, huh?" He quirked a crooked smile. "Though your timing could maybe use some work."

Caius relaxed and covered his eyes again. "'S just the brandy, that's all. Ignore me."

Decian snorted. "Ignore you getting hard for me? Bit of a tall order there, since it's been, like, a year since I last got laid. Too bad this next part is going to kill the mood stone dead. Here—bite down on this."

Caius lifted his arm enough to find Decian offering his thick leather belt, and grunted with discontent before taking it and biting down on it as ordered. The agony of strong spirits flushing out the rip in his flesh left by the crossbow bolt did, as promised, wipe every last thought of ardor from his mind. He arched and cried out around the makeshift gag, writhing until the pain subsided to more manageable levels.

He was barely aware of Decian wrapping the leg in clean linen and sliding the belt from between his gritted teeth. Cool hands lifted his head, supporting the back of his neck and holding the brandy bottle to his lips until it was empty. A wet cloth mopped at the sweat beading his forehead and chest, but somehow he was asleep before the soothing sensation truly registered.

TEN

Of course, on the one night when he truly needed some damned rest, Caius dreamed again. This was not the childhood nightmare of death in the forest. Instead, it was a soldier's dream of battle lost, and honor ground underfoot. Caius had barely turned eighteen when, fresh out of military training, he'd been sent as an oarsman to be part of the naval assault on the Eburosi port of Llanmeer.

At the time, the emperor had been set on adding the barbarian island of Eburos to his crown—a shining jewel of natural resources and productive mines that had somehow managed to cling to its independence up to that point. After the natives launched a series of ambush attacks on Alyrion troops pushing north into the wilder areas of the island, Constanzus had decided to move in with a larger force, attacking by sea.

As a freshly commissioned grunt with no battle experience, Caius had only learned the details of the assault later. At the time, he'd merely been told to row the damned boat and kill as many barbarians as he could skewer on the end of his sword once they reached the beach.

As tactics went, it had seemed straightforward enough.

Caius remembered the swell of pride he'd felt as part of the massive waves of sleek, six-man landing craft sculling through the water in well-disciplined lines. He also remembered the bewildering barrage of cloth pouches packed with rocks and choking powder raining down on their boats from lines of trebuchets arrayed along the cliff tops as they neared the shore.

Many of the pouches had burst open on impact, coating the boats and the unlucky men aboard them with fine gray dust. They hadn't understood what was happening until a salvo of flaming arrows followed the hail of powder filled pouches, and the dust-covered vessels had promptly exploded into fireballs, sinking with all aboard.

Caius had watched in disbelief as the boats surrounding him were decimated, only sheer luck keeping his afloat as other men screamed around him—burning and drowning, weighed down by their metal armor. The commanders had bellowed at the surviving men, driving them forward through the carnage of the sinking fleet and onto the shore.

The first wave to make it through had engaged the enemy barbarians on the beach, fighting their way up a rocky path carved into the cliff side to get to the city above. They were already halfway up, barbarians falling like cattle to the slaughter, when Caius' boat reached the shore and scraped to a halt against the sandy bottom. He'd barely had a chance to scramble out of the craft and draw his sword when the army of unnatural wolves had arrived.

On the voyage across the channel, the men had amused each other with tales of pagan Eburosi shapeshifters who could control the spirits of animals with magic. He'd laughed off the stories with the rest of the soldiers, pretending with a young man's bravado that they didn't chill him to his marrow... that they didn't fling his mind back to his childhood and a dead stag surrounded by the corpses of fallen guardsmen.

In the Alyrion homeland, one did not acknowledge belief in the power of pagan warlocks aloud. Not in the army. Not if one wanted to advance. Not even when one's own father had been killed by a shapeshifter.

On a beach in Eburos, however, the wolves came like a tide, ripping and tearing at Alyrion soldiers while leaving the enemy barbarians untouched... and Caius turned tail in fear, fleeing back to his boat. It would have been the most humiliating moment of his life, were it not for the fact that every other soldier still standing was doing exactly the same thing. Such cowardice during battle should have been cause for court-martial and expulsion, were it not for the fact that turning out so many soldiers at once would only have served to bring more attention to what was already a disgraceful defeat.

Caius jerked awake from a vision of two wolves closing on him as he stumbled toward his boat, his heavy armor slowing his footsteps until it felt as though he were slogging through treacle. He lay in bed, staring at the plastered cornices of his bedroom ceiling, his heart and his head pounding in time with each other.

Only when he tried to swing into a sitting position did the recent past swim into focus. His thigh screamed a protest at the movement. He swallowed a curse as he fell back — remembering the hunt, and the would-be assassins in the forest.

Remembering *Decian*.

The light filtering in through the window held the gray, uncertain quality of early morning. Caius took a deep breath and sat up more carefully this time, clutching his bandaged leg to steady it. His head protested the change in elevation... or, more accurately, it protested the amount of brandy he'd swigged the previous evening. He ignored the pounding ache, taking stock of the rest of his body as best he could.

The arm wasn't too bad. It had scabbed well while he slept, and since he already favored that arm as a matter of course, he was used to the restriction in movement that would be necessary to protect the wound for a few days. The leg would be more of a hindrance — but only a small amount of blood had seeped through the bandages overnight, and he was able to cautiously bend and straighten his knee without anything catastrophic happening.

The rest of his body felt like he'd run headlong through a forest full of underbrush and fought two men half his age. Which... was reasonable under the circumstances, he supposed. At least he'd fought two men half his age and *won*.

He let his gaze wander around the room, unsurprised to find it empty of anyone except him.

Cautiously, he stretched the parts of himself that hadn't been recently injured, and levered himself onto his good leg. A bit of experimentation proved that as long as he was careful, the bad one would take his weight without buckling. With slow, hitching steps, he hobbled to the chamberpot and relieved himself.

As he was lacing up his smallclothes, he heard a shuffle of movement coming from the front of the house and stilled. Had someone informed Tertia that he'd been injured? The slave woman wouldn't normally be here to perform her duties until midday, and frankly, Caius couldn't picture her rushing to his bedside just because he'd taken a crossbow bolt to the leg.

Out of an abundance of caution, he limped to the side table and reached for his swordbelt. He'd just pulled the blade from its sheath when Decian wandered in with a hunk of bread piled with cheese held halfway to his mouth. He froze in the doorway when he saw the sword.

"Er... good morning?" he hazarded. "I assume this either means you're feeling better, or you're really, *really* unhappy with my bandaging job for some reason."

Caius let out a sharp breath and sheathed the sword. "I thought you'd gone."

"Oh, I did," Decian told him, taking a bite of the bread and cheese and pausing to chew before speaking around it. "I've been in and out a few times, making sure Pip was doing all right on his own with the dogs, and letting him know what was going on." He swallowed. "I met your house servant yesterday afternoon. Tertia, I think she said her name was? She's very... what's the word? Oh, yes. *Terrifying*."

Caius snorted and sank back on the bed. Someone—either Decian or Tertia, presumably—had left a goblet of water on the table for him, sitting next to the swordbelt. He reached for it and drained it dry, knowing it would help with his head.

"Oh, she's fine, really," he said. "The trick is to avoid her completely. Though I have no doubt she'd say the same thing about me."

Decian smiled his crooked smile. "Well, she left you enough food for a small army, and said to tell you she'd be back around midday today. You should probably eat—I can bring you something, if you'd like?"

The way Caius' stomach protested the idea told him he probably *should* eat, if only to soak up the remnants of the brandy. He scrubbed a hand over his face, rubbing at his eyes. "Bread and cheese would be good, yes. And some more water, as well. Thank you."

Decian nodded and disappeared, leaving Caius to contemplate what it was about this situation that had him feeling so off-balance. Then he remembered the part where he'd nearly poked Decian's eye out with his erection while the poor man had been preparing to clean his wound.

Oh.

Yes... that would certainly account for it. Even more so, since Decian hadn't seemed put off by the idea at all.

His traitorous cock stirred with interest at the memory, just as Decian returned with a fresh slab of bread and a goblet. Caius ignored his body's distraction and accepted the simple meal with gruff thanks. Once he started eating, his vague sense of queasiness transformed into ravenous hunger— unsurprising, since he hadn't eaten anything in slightly over a day.

When he was done, he set the second empty goblet alongside the first and contemplated what to do next.

"You should rest more, if you can," Decian said, as though in answer to his thoughts. "Oh, and I should probably change that bandage before I head out again. You bled through it."

"I can take care of it." He didn't mean for the words to sound so brusque.

Decian lifted his eyes skyward. "Or I could take care of it, since I have equal use of both my arms and I'm here anyway."

For the second time in twenty-four hours, Caius found himself being pushed bodily onto his back on the bed, his bad leg lifted up to rest on the feather-stuffed mattress. And this time, he wasn't fighting post-battle shock and exhaustion.

Though his leg still hurt like damnation, blast it all.

The pain wasn't enough to keep his arousal at bay when deft hands unwrapped the linen cloth from around his thigh. Decian shot him a wry smile.

"And you can't even blame the brandy this time," he quipped.

"Maybe I can't," Caius shot back, taking in Decian's dilated pupils... the way his tongue darted out to wet his lower lip. "But what's your excuse?"

Dark eyes met his, unafraid and unapologetic. "Told you already. It's been a while for me—no mystery there." He blinked, and turned his gaze determinedly to the wound as he lifted the last layer of linen away. "Hmm... that seems to be doing decently well, all things considered. It's pretty swollen—"

"That's normal," Caius said.

" —but it doesn't smell like it's festering, and it seems to have clotted nicely," Decian finished. "Shall I flush it again?"

Caius waved him off. "No. Just bandage it, please. As long as the wound stays sound, there's no point in doing anything more to it. You'll only start it bleeding again."

"Hmm. You're the expert, I suppose." Decian retrieved fresh linen and rewrapped the wound, tucking the ends in and checking to make sure it wasn't too tight or too loose. Satisfied, he let his fingertips trail along the smallclothes covering Caius' inner thigh and brush over the length resting hard and heavy at the apex. "And now, I should probably leave before I'm tempted to take advantage of an injured man."

A jolt of raw lust sparked up Caius' spine in response the soft stroke of fingers. Before Decian could do more than yelp in surprise, Caius grabbed him by the shirtfront with his good arm and jerked him onto the bed, rolling them until Decian was on his back with Caius next to him, looking down at his startled expression. His leg and arm barked an indignant protest at the sudden movement. He ignored the flare of pain in favor of fusing his lips to Decian's, swallowing his gasp of surprise.

ELEVEN

Caius fumbled with the younger man's trouser laces right-handed, tugging and burrowing until his fingers closed around hard flesh, freeing Decian's cock from layers of clothing. Decian thrust up helplessly into the circle of Caius' fist, making a muffled, desperate noise into the kiss. Caius jerked him fast and hard and without finesse, not letting up with either lips or hand until Decian arched and came silently, spilling over Caius' fingers and his own clothing.

He gentled his movements as Decian shuddered beneath his touch, taking a moment to appreciate the length and weight of the other man's cock as it twitched a few more times and began to soften. With a final nip to Decian's lower lip, Caius pulled away from the kiss, but kept a proprietary grip wrapped lightly around his spent prick.

"Word to the wise," he said. "Never tease a soldier — even a wounded one."

Decian blinked up at the ceiling with dazed, unfocused eyes. Caius could see his pulse jumping beneath his jaw. His own cock throbbed with insistent need despite the pain from his leg. He ignored both sensations in favor of enjoying the view in front of him.

After a long moment, Decian swallowed, his throat bobbing. "Oh... I dunno," he said slowly, rolling his head to the side until he could meet Caius' gaze. "I feel as though it's working out rather well for me, so far."

Caius huffed out a startled breath of laughter, the impulse taking him by surprise.

Decian eyed him speculatively, a smile tugging at one corner of his full lips. "The problem is, I've no idea what I can do to reciprocate that won't end up jarring your leg in the process."

Caius raised an eyebrow at him. "Simple. You can lie back and look appealingly debauched for a few more minutes."

He let go of Decian's prick with a last slow stroke, enjoying the full-body shiver it elicited. With great deliberation, he untied the closure of his undergarment and took himself in hand, his fingers still slick with Decian's release. Decian caught his breath.

With a grunt, Caius levered himself into a more upright position to reduce the strain on his bad arm. He still ached all over after the previous day's abuse... but he was damned if that was going to stop him spilling his seed all over the sated man currently sprawled in his bed.

"*God*, you're beautiful when you've just come," he said, working himself steadily—feeling the exquisite tension gathering at the base of his spine, despite the discomfort clamoring elsewhere in his body.

"You're not so bad when you're getting ready to come, either," Decian said. "Keep going." He looked up with luminous eyes, his gaze traveling with leisurely slowness between Caius' face and his hand working his own flesh.

It had been an embarrassingly long time since Caius had been with anyone who didn't expect payment afterward. In the back of his mind, he was acutely aware that the emperor's bastard son was just about the most foolish choice of bed partner he could possibly have made. Yet, somehow his impetuous decision to save Decian in the first place appeared to have opened the floodgates when it came to making foolish choices that were also the *right* choices.

Decian's lazy half-smile turned wicked. The same clever fingers that had teased him earlier and precipitated all of this snuck between them and closed over Caius' grip on his own prick, guiding his movements. Decian's thumb swiped over the engorged head on the upstroke, sliding through the moisture beading there.

Pleasure punched hard into Caius' gut, cresting and spilling. He gritted his teeth, his cock pulsing in hot spurts that did, indeed, make his leg hurt like hell as his body jerked through the release. Thin ropes of pearly white splattered across Decian's softening prick and open trousers. Finally spent, Caius managed a marginally controlled collapse onto his back, lying shoulder to shoulder with the other man.

"Bloody hellfire," he muttered, as post-coital lassitude leached all the pain from his body, leaving him feeling limp as a used washrag.

Decian lay just as spent, his arm flopping down to lie at his side. "No respect for clothing," he said, sounding half-amused and half-exasperated. "That's your problem. Look at this mess. These trousers aren't even mine, you know."

Caius choked on another breath of laughter, even though the reminder of the dead houndsman should have been anything but humorous. "There's all the clean water you could want in the fountain. Sponge them off before the spunk dries, and no one will know the difference." He waved an uncoordinated hand in the air. "I'd offer to do it for you, but…" He indicated his compromised state.

"You're an injured man," Decian finished for him. "Yes, I can see that. Practically at death's door. It's tragic, really."

Caius nodded in sage agreement and let his eyes slip closed. "S'right," he agreed, and grunted when a lithe body crawled over him to get to the side of the bed, being careful not to jar his leg in the process.

He was on the cusp of dozing when Decian returned a few minutes later and crawled over him again, settling with his back against the headboard this time. Vague surprise motivated Caius to peel open one eye and peer at him curiously.

"What?" Decian asked. He indicated his damp trousers. "I'm sorry, but I'm not in much of a hurry to go outside looking like I've just pissed myself. Besides, your bed is *really comfortable*."

"It's too soft," he protested.

Decian made a disbelieving noise. "I recognize those words you're using, but they don't make any sense when you put them together in that order. How can a mattress be 'too soft'?"

"I spent too much time sleeping on hard pallets and tattered bedrolls in the army," he muttered. "It's what I'm used to."

Decian huffed. "And I spent ten years sleeping on dirty straw in a prison cell. What's your point?"

"I don't belong on a feather bed," Caius mumbled, slipping toward the siren call of slumber despite his best efforts. "Don't belong... in this place." Something important occurred to him in the instant before he would have drifted off with a man lying next to him in his bed. "Tertia—"

"Your house slave won't be here for hours yet," Decian reminded him. "Don't worry, O mighty soldier. Your virtue is safe with me. Safer than mine is with you, it appears."

"Oh. That's all right, then," Caius decided, and promptly fell asleep. This time, he didn't dream.

>••~ ⚜ ~••<

He wasn't sure if it was the sound of voices that woke him next, or the glare of sunlight in his eyes. He grunted and turned his head away, trying to escape the stabbing beam. It was early afternoon... apparently. Caius wasn't in the habit of being in bed at this time of day, and whoever had designed the windows in the house clearly agreed that use of the bedroom for sleeping after midday was something to be discouraged in the strongest possible terms.

It was, he reflected, a bit worrying that he'd slept through whatever conversation was taking place outside the room. He recognized both voices, and while neither of them belonged to anyone he considered a threat, the idea of both of them together did engender a faint sense of dread in the pit of his stomach.

Thankfully, he retained the presence of mind to check whether his smallclothes were laced up before he levered himself out of bed and went hobbling outside to confront the owners of the voices... because they weren't. His underclothes were, in fact, hanging obscenely open. He fumbled them into order with clumsy fingers, cursing the stiffness of his left arm.

Maybe he should have worried more about the propriety of wandering out to confront his middle-aged house slave while bare-chested and trouserless, but in truth, Caius doubted there was much he could do at this point that would lower Tertia's opinion of him any further than it already was.

He limped out to the enclosed garden, drawing the attention of both Tertia and Decian, who were conversing at the mouth of the hallway leading through to the atrium.

"You can go home, Tertia," he said, in lieu of a greeting. "You don't need to be here."

Tertia eyed him up and down, lifting her chin as she pinned him with an unimpressed gaze. Her iron gray hair was escaping its bun as it often did. Her unadorned stola had been stained dark at the bottom, as though the edge had fallen into a mop-bucket at some point in the recent past. Her mouth turned down at the corners, accentuating the wrinkles in her careworn face.

"Pompous fool," she said. "Go back to bed. Do you not have the sense Deimok gave a snail?" Then she turned back to Decian, dismissing Caius' presence as effectively as if she'd closed an invisible door in his face.

Caius felt his jaw tighten.

"I'm not an invalid, Tertia," he told her.

This time, her gray eyes flashed with irritation when she looked at him. "You're standing in the garden in your underclothes and keeping yourself upright by holding onto the wall, *Legatus*. Now, go back to bed before I pour a tincture down your throat that will put you out like a snuffed candle, and keep you out for the rest of the day."

Decian choked on a laugh and tried, unconvincingly, to turn it into a cough. Caius glared at him, the traitor.

"I'm going back to my room now," he said, with all the dignity he could muster. "But only because it's a more appealing prospect than continuing this conversation."

"I couldn't agree more," Tertia said. "I'll have Decian bring you bone broth and bread dipped in oil in a bit. Try to avoid getting in the way of any more arrows until then, eh?"

Caius gritted his teeth. "Tell you what. I'll do that, if you try to avoid acting like an objectionable old crone."

Tertia grinned at him, revealing crooked teeth. "I *am* an objectionable old crone," she retorted. "Which is still better than being a pompous fool. Oh, and by the way — the workmen will be here the day after tomorrow to repair the broken roof tiles from the storm last week. I told them what they were originally trying to charge was highway robbery, so they're doing it for half that."

"It's a source of amazement to me that any artisans are willing to work on this place at all, after dealing with you," Caius said.

"You're welcome," she told him, and pointedly turned back to Decian again.

Caius sighed and hobbled back to his room, defeated.

When Decian showed up some time later with two bowls of broth and a plate of sliced bread balanced on a tray, Caius was seated on the bed, sharpening his dagger with a whetstone. His sword hung in its scabbard, freshly cleaned and oiled after being bloodied by an assassin's entrails. Decian put the tray down carefully on the small table next to the bed and gave the dagger a pointed look.

"Tertia said she was leaving for the day and would be back in the morning. Out of curiosity, if you two really hate each other that much, why not get a different house slave?" he asked.

"Too much effort," Caius replied succinctly, not pausing in his brisk movements as the stone scraped rhythmically along the blade. "Besides, she keeps the floors clean."

"And saves money on roof repairs, I gather," Decian offered. "And makes sure you don't starve."

"That, too."

Decian took a slice of bread and one of the bowls before settling on the floor, his back resting against the side of the bed next to Caius' good leg.

He dipped the bread in the broth and bit into it. Caius tried not to let the younger man's proximity distract him from his foul mood. He flipped the knife over and started work on the other edge.

"You know," Decian said around a mouthful, "There was a prisoner in the cell across from mine who managed to snap a piece off one of the door hinges where it had rusted partway through. He spent almost six months trying to sharpen that hunk of iron into a blade. *Scrape, scrape, scrape,* every night until I thought I'd go mad. He'd almost managed to get an edge on the damned thing when the guards found it and took it away. I always found that ironic. That's the right word, isn't it? Ironic?"

"Sounds right," Caius agreed, drawing the blade across the stone at an angle. "What happened to him afterward?"

"They beat him to a bloody pulp as an example to the rest of us. The broken fingers on his right hand never healed properly, and he could barely see out of his left eye when they were done with him. But at least the infernal scraping stopped."

"Do you think one of the other prisoners ratted him out?" Caius asked absently. He set the blade and whetstone on the table, in favor of taking up the second bowl and a hunk of the coarse bread.

"No idea," Decian replied. He jerked his chin toward the dagger resting next to the tray. "Are you expecting to fight off any more assassins in the near future?"

Caius scowled, focusing intently on his broth. "Not likely. That was the first real action I've seen in four years." And somehow, in the aftermath of that ugly two-on-one struggle, he'd never felt less at home inside the safety of the palace compound. "Like I said before, I don't belong in this place. I was never cut out to be a palace lapdog."

"Believe it or not, I can relate to that," Decian said, and took another bite of broth-soaked bread. He gestured around the room with the bitten piece. "Still. Nice digs."

Caius let out a breath of startled amusement. "I suppose so." He tipped the bowl to his lips, swallowing the contents and mopping up the dregs with the crust of bread before setting it back on the tray.

In truth, no amount of cleaning and polishing his weapons would erase the reality of the last four years. His soldiering days were over, and the odds of a repeat of the scene in the forest were about as likely as the odds of Proclus giving up drinking wine in favor of water. Frankly, it was a miracle he'd fared as well as he had against two younger opponents armed with crossbows.

"So... I was thinking this morning," Decian began.

"Always dangerous," Caius observed, battling his own memories of the morning. Specifically, the way the morning light had outlined his sated companion's body as he lay sprawled across this very bed.

"I was thinking that I could get used to having enough to eat and a place to stay that doesn't have a door made of iron bars," Decian continued, oblivious. "I could get used to having money and a job to do. You know?"

Unease coiled in Caius' gut, twining together with something lighter. Something hopeful.

"Staying in the palace grounds would be dangerous for you," he said carefully.

Decian craned around to meet his gaze. "Oh, yes? What happened to 'no one cares who feeds the dogs as long as the dogs get fed'?"

"That was before Kaeto showed an interest in you," Caius told him.

Decian's dark brows drew together. "He asked who I was. And then immediately got distracted. Which, I might add, is exactly how someone behaves when they don't actually care about the answer to the question they just asked."

"Even so—" Caius began.

"Am I right in thinking that after yesterday's debacle, there aren't likely to be any royal hunts requiring use of the hounds for a while?" Decian pressed.

Not unless the emperor descends even further into madness than he already has, Caius thought. Aloud, he only said, "Probably not."

"There you go, then."

Caius scowled. "And if Kaeto shows up at the kennels with another prisoner slated for execution-by-hound?"

Decian's expression hardened. "Then I'll hold the dogs off him and sneak him out the back when no one's looking." He raised an eyebrow. "It's a trick I just learned recently, you know?"

The sinking feeling in Caius' stomach grew. So did his selfish desire not to see the last of the emperor's half-Kulawi bastard son, who could control ravenous hounds with a look and who smiled so sweetly after spilling his seed over Caius' hand.

"It's a horrible idea," Caius said. "Really, truly horrible."

Decian raised an eyebrow. "Well, you could always turn me in as an escaped prisoner if it bothers you so much."

Caius snorted. "Right. And then I could explain how I mistook the houndsman's dismembered corpse for yours, and you for him."

"Good point," Decian acknowledged. "Best not, I suppose." A slow smile tugged at one corner of his lips. "Besides, if you did turn me in, you'd never find out what it's like to fuck me when you don't have a bleeding hole in your leg."

And just like that, the blood was rushing to Caius' cock again, as though he were a callow youth rather than a used-up soldier well into his fifth decade. He forced his body under control, and his expression to blandness.

"This is just an observation, mind," he said. "But when trying to convince an imperial advisor that the risk related to your staying in the palace grounds is negligible, offering to become his secret male lover in nearly the same breath doesn't really do much to bolster your argument."

Decian tilted his head, regarding Caius curiously. "This place has some seriously twisted views on sex. Just saying." He set his empty bowl on the floor and rested an elbow on the bed. "Doesn't that ever bother you?"

Caius shrugged. "It is what it is."

"Things are very different where my mother came from."

"Kulawi?" Caius hazarded.

Decian nodded. "There, they don't judge people for who they sleep with. As long as everyone involved is an adult and agrees of their own free will, who cares? What does it matter to anyone else?"

Caius wondered how Decian, of all people, could ask that. "It matters plenty to any man who needs an heir," he said, thinking of the steady stream of imperial bastards who *hadn't* escaped execution at Kaeto's hands.

But Decian only scoffed. "This may come as a shock to you, but I'm extremely unlikely to get you pregnant, *Legatus*. Or vice versa."

"That's not what I meant and you know it. If a woman can lie with anyone, then how can a man's title and property pass to his sons?"

"That's simple enough," Decian retorted wryly. "In Kulawi, wealth passes through the mother. That part is surprisingly easy to keep track of, no matter who's sleeping with who."

Caius blinked at him, trying to wrap his mind around the concept and failing.

"My point is," Decian went on, "I don't give two shits about what people in Alyrios think about sex." He gave Caius a long, assessing look. "And if *you* do—frankly, you've got a really strange way of showing it."

TWELVE

There wasn't much to say to that, since Caius had shamelessly fucked his fair share of fellow soldiers in the army, not to mention seeking out a prostitute in Amarius willing to cater to... multiple tastes, so to speak.

"I care enough not to advertise the fact in the middle of the Alyrion capital," he managed.

Decian exhaled sharply. "Well, it *would* be a pity to get yourself excommunicated and lose this lovely house, I'm sure."

"It would also be a pity to end up getting stoned in the streets by a jeering mob," Caius retorted.

"Agreed," Decian said. "I'm not a big proponent of gruesome execution, as you may have guessed. All of which makes me wonder why you'd choose to risk it in the first place? Why not find yourself a nice young widow to marry, and avoid tumbling random men into bed in the future? Problem solved, surely."

"I had a wife once."

The words hung in the air, surprising Caius since he certainly hadn't meant to say them aloud. Decian twisted his upper body to regard him more directly, resting his chin on his forearm at the edge of the too-soft feather mattress.

"Oh? What happened to her?" His tone made it clear that he'd picked up the subtext beneath Caius' use of the past tense.

"She… died in childbirth." Again, the words seemed to be pulled from him, rather than exiting his lips voluntarily. "She was twenty-one. I was twenty-three. We'd been trying for more than three years. It was her first pregnancy."

His voice sounded… not like him.

Decian must have noticed as well. "You loved her?"

He swallowed. Nodded. "I did. It was an arranged marriage, but we were well matched." With a jolt, he realized that at age forty-six, he'd lived exactly half his life since Serah and their infant daughter had died. "I'd like to think she loved me as well," he finished.

Silence settled for a long moment before Decian spoke again. "And in the time since, you never considered marrying again?"

An unwelcome vision of Serah's pale, sweat-soaked face as she labored to bring a dead child into the world before it killed her flickered through his memory, and Caius shook his head slowly.

"No."

He had no desire to risk such a thing a second time. It was much easier to tumble the occasional soldier or prostitute when the need for companionship became too distracting.

Decian stared up at him with a somber expression. "I shouldn't have jested about pregnancy earlier. Forgive me."

But Caius waved him off with an irritated flick of the hand. "Don't be ridiculous. It was decades ago."

The room descended into thoughtful silence once more. Caius found himself studying Decian's dark eyes... his sleek black helmet of closely shorn hair... the noble line of his Alyrion cheekbones and jaw paired with a nose that was wider and flatter than was usual in this land. He had to consciously stop himself brushing his own lips with his fingers as the echo of the kisses he'd stolen from Decian tingled along the skin.

Decian's gaze dipped to his mouth as though he were somehow privy to those private thoughts. The tip of his tongue darted out to wet his full lips, and his gaze lifted to meet Caius' again.

"I need to get back to the kennels," he said. "Is the bandage all right? I can check it again before I leave."

Caius took a slow breath and let it out silently, dragging his wandering thoughts under control. "No, leave it. It's fine — better to disturb the wound as little as possible unless it starts to fester."

Decian nodded and made to rise. "Fair enough. You've already proven you can get around if you need to, but I'll bring a jug of watered wine and a plate of food in here for you to eat later so you don't have to get up. You'll be all right on your own for the rest of the day?"

A small smile tugged at one corner of Caius' mouth, though he covered it out of old habit. "I've managed this long. I expect I'll survive until tomorrow."

He looked up as Decian moved to stand in front of him, unused to being seated while someone else loomed over him. Decian reached out a hard-callused hand and tipped Caius' jaw up with a gentle touch, thumb playing over his cheekbone and leaving a trail of heat in its wake.

"See that you do," Decian told him.

It was several days before Caius' leg recovered enough for him to walk unaided, without the need for something or someone to lean on. By that time, he was slowly going mad with boredom despite regular visits from Decian and Tertia. Every blade in the house was sharp enough to split a hair, whether its intended use was the battlefield or the kitchen.

On the fourth day, an administrator from the palace had showed up at his door to inquire about his health. The man took one look at Caius balancing his weight against the doorframe and told him he would inform His Imperial Majesty that the legatus needed more time to recover before returning to his duties at court.

Caius had bristled, ready to snap that he was as capable of standing in the corner and being ignored with an injured leg as with a sound one. He stopped himself, realizing with a jolt that he had absolutely no interest in returning to his duties before he was forced to do so. As much as it went against his nature to malinger, the truth was that he had taken a moderately serious injury in defense of the imperial family. If recovering meant he would be spared a front row seat to the slow dissolution of the empire for a few more days...

It wasn't an unappealing prospect, even with the associated boredom.

On the eighth morning, Decian showed up at the house with an air of purpose. He let himself in without knocking, as he'd grown accustomed to doing over the past few visits.

"Get dressed for riding," he called. "We're taking the dogs out for a run. I had a stableboy bring your horse along." He poked his head into the bedroom as he spoke the last few words, a broad smile gracing his attractive features.

Caius felt his mood lighten at the prospect. This, despite his nagging, ever-present pall of worry related to Decian's decision to stay on as royal houndsman rather than fleeing to obscurity in the hills.

"Oh? Are we indeed?" he asked, lifting a skeptical eyebrow — mostly for the form of the thing.

"Yes we are," Decian said with finality. "I didn't manage to acquire a winch to help get you into the saddle, but I expect we can muddle through somehow."

"Arse," Caius said without heat. Already, he was relishing the thought of leaving the confines of his house. For one thing, the walls had been closing in on him at odd moments lately whenever his thoughts began spinning in tight circles.

"Come on, now... you don't want to miss the spectacle of me bouncing around on that damned pony's back like a fool, do you?" Decian teased.

Caius let out a breath of laughter. "Well, when you put it like that…"

"So get dressed," Decian insisted. "Do you need help?"

The flare of stubbornness that prickled along Caius' spine was probably misplaced, but he'd spent enough time feeling like an invalid in the past few days.

"No, I am actually capable of dressing myself, thank you," he said tartly. "I'll join you in a few minutes."

Decian shrugged agreement and went out to wait for him.

Fortunately for Caius' pride, he was able to successfully pull on his riding breeches and boots without making too much of a hash of things. Which wasn't to say the process was painless—it very much wasn't. At this point, however, he was happy to bear a bit of pain as long as it meant getting back to something closer to normalcy.

When did riding out with the palace houndsman to exercise the dogs ever constitute normalcy?

Caius scowled at the unwelcome prodding of his niggling internal voice. Riding was normal, he told himself firmly. Getting out of the blasted house was normal. The details of where, why, and with whom were irrelevant.

He limped outside to find Decian and the stableboy waiting for him. His gray gelding tossed its head and nickered, lifting one front foot to paw at the cobbles. Beside it, the apathetic roan pony dozed in the sun, muzzle drooping and one hind leg cocked at the hip. Both animals' saddles were hung with waterskins, and the pony carried a pair of bulging saddlebags as well.

Decian looked Caius up and down critically. "Hmm. Looks like you were telling the truth. Boots on the correct feet... breeches laced up... shirt on the right way around. I concede that you are, in fact, able to dress yourself. Ready to go?"

Caius caught the stableboy's look of bug-eyed horror at seeing someone speak to a palace advisor — an imperial legatus — in such a way. He scowled at Decian because it was expected of him.

"I may owe you for helping when I was injured, houndsman," he said with mock severity. "But someday soon, someone's going to shove something in that smart mouth of yours to shut you up."

He saw the double entendre hit home — saw Decian cover a smirk, and caught the faint darkening of his brown eyes.

"Many have threatened," he replied in a tone of amusement. "Yet here we stand, bantering. Let's get you mounted. How would be best?"

Caius greeted the gelding, rubbing his mount's muzzle affectionately before gathering up the reins and facing the saddle. "A leg-up should suffice... if you've got the shoulders for it."

"Didn't I tell you we'd muddle through?" Decian teased. "So, how do I — oh, I see."

Caius bent his bad leg at the knee and Decian cupped it in both hands, heaving upward at the same time Caius pushed off with his good right leg and pulled himself up with his right arm. The maneuver was every bit as painful as dressing himself had been, but Decian was strong and Caius had been scrambling onto horses' backs since he was knee-high to one. With a grunt of effort and a bit of shuffling, he was in the saddle. He settled himself into place, fished around for the stirrups, and arranged the reins in his right hand.

"I have him now, lad," he told the boy, who'd been steadying the gray's head during the inelegant mounting process.

Decian clambered onto the pony with approximately the same lack of grace Caius had just demonstrated. The aging beast snorted awake and rolled a baleful eye at his rider before yawning widely.

"Maybe I'll train a couple of the dogs to pull me around in a cart and save both of us the trouble, you horrible little beast," Decian muttered, fumbling with the reins one handed and reaching down with the other to twist the offside stirrup leather so he could get his foot into it.

"That I'd like to see," Caius said. He flipped a coin into the stableboy's waiting hands and urged his gelding into motion. Decian kicked his heels into the pony's ribs a couple of times and followed him.

The scab across Caius' upper arm was barely a hindrance at this point, though his bad shoulder was not expressing much appreciation for the recent stretch of inactivity. Meanwhile, his injured leg ached and throbbed in time with the easy movement of the horse beneath him. It was, he knew from long experience, the kind of pain that would diminish as his flesh continued to knit itself back together. Not the kind that warned of further damage being done to a fresh wound.

Decian jounced along next to him, glancing over to meet his eyes. "So, are you truly feeling better, or just putting a brave face on it?"

"It's an annoyance at this point; nothing more," Caius assured him. He tried not to think about how much faster he'd healed from similar injuries a decade ago... much less *two* decades ago.

"Well, whatever you do, don't fall off. If you do, I'll make you ride the pony so I don't have to heft you onto that monster's back again."

Caius' lips twitched. "That assumes you'd have any more luck climbing onto this *monster's* back than I would, after that performance to mount the pony. Now... look here. You're holding the reins like you're driving a plow horse. Hold them like this instead, but with one rein in each hand."

He lifted his right hand, demonstrating the rein position. Decian studied it and changed his own grip to match.

"Better," Caius said. "Now lower your hands. Keep them close to the pommel—that's the front of the saddle. Only move one of them at a time when you need to steer. Set your hips and squeeze your fists closed to slow or stop. Though honestly, I expect you could just stop kicking him in the sides. That would work, too, since I'm fairly certain that pony's default speed is 'asleep.'"

"I'm fairly certain you're right," Decian grumbled.

They made their way through the palace grounds to the royal kennels, with Caius offering occasional tips and corrections to address the more egregious points of Decian's riding form.

"I'm going to be sore for a week," the younger man complained. "Which isn't something you'll have much sympathy for, I suppose."

"It comes with the territory," Caius told him. "Competence on horseback requires hundreds of hours spent in the saddle."

"Hmm. Sounds awful," Decian said, just as the pony gave an irritated little cow-kick.

Pip was waiting to meet them in the kennel courtyard, surrounded by two-dozen excited hounds whose shoulders came up past the level of his waist. "They're ready for a good run," he said by way of greeting, offering Caius a wary dip of his head in acknowledgement. "Do you know the fields east of the river gate, sir? That's where Jona always used to take them for exercise."

"I do," Caius assured him. The area was used for grazing by many of the freemen with smallholdings outside the city, but only during winter. It was a good place for a gallop—or for running a pack.

"Lead on, in that case," Decian said. "Pip, after the kennels are clean, feel free to take a few hours for yourself. We'll be back by mid-afternoon."

Pip brightened. "All right. I will, thanks."

Decian smiled at him, open and easy. "Enjoy… but don't get into trouble. See you later."

He gave a low whistle, and the dogs trotted toward him, surrounding the bored-looking pony. Caius steadied his own mount, who wasn't quite so accustomed to being hemmed in by predators at close range.

"This way," he said, and headed toward the river gate.

THIRTEEN

The eastern fields stretched across hundreds of *arpennes* of gently rolling hills bounded by forest. The place was peaceful and empty, which suited Caius well. It wasn't so much the bustle of the city that he'd missed while cooped up in his rooms, as it was the open sky and a sense of freedom. Decian was as agreeable a companion as one could ask for, and the dogs were eerily well behaved as they trotted along, tongues lolling, sniffing the air occasionally.

"I trust they can get their exercise without us needing to keep pace with them the whole time," Caius said wryly.

Decian might be acquiring a basic grasp of steering and changing the pony's speed, but he still had no kind of seat. And Caius had no desire to test his leg's mettle at a faster gait unless he was forced to do so.

"I think they're going to have to," Decian replied in the same dry tone. He pulled a curled hunting horn from his saddle as they approached the top of a hill—one that gave a good view of the grasslands stretching all around. Lifting the horn to his lips, he blew two short blasts, and the dogs exploded forward in a riot of excited baying.

"And away they go," Caius mused, enjoying the play of the sleek hounds' muscles as they raced down the hill, leaping and jostling with each other.

"They needed this today," Decian said, watching them indulgently.

So did I, Caius thought.

They watched together until the dogs wore themselves out. Decian redirected them with the sound of the hunting horn whenever they threatened to wander too far away. Eventually, they began to return to their master, panting and bright-eyed. Once the whole pack had rejoined them, Caius led the way toward a stream that ran along one of the wooded boundaries. The dogs and horses sated their thirst, several of the hounds splashing noisily into the water to cool off.

"Is that food in your saddlebags, I hope?" Caius asked.

Decian nodded. "It is. Hungry?"

"I could eat." Caius cautiously tested his thigh muscles to see how they were faring, and looked around to catalogue their immediate surroundings. Satisfied, he swung his good leg over the front of the saddle and slid down slowly, landing with his weight on his right foot.

"*Hey*. Didn't I warned you about getting down?" Decian protested.

"You warned me about *falling off*, which I don't intend to dignify with a response." Caius gestured to a fallen tree trunk nearby. "There's a downed log I can use to mount again when it's time to leave. Don't fuss."

Decian looked skeptical, but he did step down from his pony, wincing as his feet hit the ground. "*Oww.*"

"Don't whine, either," Caius told him.

"The bottom of my spine is in imminent danger of poking through the fabric of my trouser seat after the pounding it's just taken. I'll whine if I want to, thanks."

Caius hid a smile. "You'll live."

"You think so? Well, I suppose that's more than could be said about me a couple of weeks ago." Decian stretched gingerly from side to side, his vertebrae popping audibly.

It was a sobering reminder of Decian's situation, but Caius tried not to let it spoil his pleasant mood. He led his gelding over to a tree with a sturdy branch just above head height and tied him there, showing Decian how to use a slipknot that wouldn't tighten if the animal startled and pulled back. When both mounts were settled and the dogs had flopped down around the clearing to rest in the dappled sunlight, Caius joined Decian by the downed tree. He carefully eased himself to sit on the ground, resting his back against the sturdy log and stretching his bad leg out in front of him to ease it. Decian sank down next to him with food and drink, sitting shoulder to shoulder.

They shared cold salted meat and brown bread, soft cheese and an early apple that Caius sliced into pieces with his dagger. The fact that it was the most pleasant morning he'd passed since coming to Amarius almost four years ago was something he didn't care to dwell on.

"This is nice," Decian said, echoing his thoughts. "Really, *really* nice. Do you know how long it's been since I had a day like this?" He let his head fall back against the log, looking up at the sky through the thin covering of overhanging branches. His expression grew far away.

"More than ten years?" Caius offered.

"Yes. More than ten years," Decian confirmed, rolling his head to the side to meet Caius' eyes. "Thank you for this."

"Don't thank me," Caius told him. "If it was up to me, you would have left Amarius already. You could leave right now, in fact. We're outside the city. No one's around to see you go."

Decian let out a little huff of laughter. "I'm not leaving yet. For one thing, if I tried to make a run for it now, I'd have a pack of royal hunting hounds stuck to my tail." His expression grew serious. "And for another, I'm not ready to give *this* up."

He leaned forward, and Caius felt a small jolt go through him as their lips brushed together. His eyes slipped closed, his entire focus narrowing to that slow slide of skin against sensitive skin.

It was gentle. Easy. The kind of kiss traded by young sweethearts in the first flush of attraction. It made Caius' chest hurt, but not with the sort of pain that would convince him to stop. Pursuing this dalliance was the worst kind of foolishness. He knew it in his bones... yet he made no move to pull away. Decian's lips were a drug—a sweet herbalist's concoction that made warmth and lassitude crawl through Caius' veins, unknotting his muscles and soothing his nerves. He never wanted to move from this spot... never wanted this day to end.

They were in the open, some distant part of him tried to warn. *Anyone could ride by and see them kissing, see their hands wandering in slow caresses.*

But the dogs would warn them if anyone approached. There was no track or road leading past the area. The likelihood of anyone else coming this way was small. And it had been far too long since Caius had kissed anyone like this.

He ran his fingers through the closely trimmed spirals and waves of Decian's unusual hair. It was softer than he'd expected, springing back from his touch as he stroked it. Decian made a low noise of enjoyment into the kiss. His full lips wandered to Caius' jaw, then lower — following the tendon that ran down the side of his neck.

It was such a simple touch, but Caius *felt* it... felt more than he had in years... felt so much that it hurt with a pain to rival an arrow through the leg. *God*, how had he lived for so long without *feeling*? He clutched at Decian's shoulder, at the back of his head, as though Decian were somehow in danger of leaving and taking this raw sensation of awareness with him. A choked noise wrenched free from his throat as Decian laved his collarbone, nosing aside the loose collar of his shirt.

He trailed lower still, kissing through fabric, pulling Caius' good leg to the side to make room for himself without jostling his injury overmuch. As he settled in, Caius became instantly, desperately aware of his cock pressed hard against the lacing of his breeches, throbbing with need. His fingertips kneaded the nape of Decian's neck as the younger man freed Caius' hard length from his clothing. Mission accomplished, he settled his body in the soft grass between Caius' legs.

The first touch of Decian's lips and tongue to his cockhead was so intense, so *immediate* that it drove every other thought from his head. It was cool water after a trek through the desert; a warm bath after hours spent in the cold. It was the sight of camp after a battle hard-won. It was home after a long journey.

He stroked that soft, springy helmet of hair, letting his head fall back as Decian's lips slid down his shaft with confidence, tongue swirling in complicated patterns against his skin. Leaves rustled above him in the light breeze, the sound of birds competing with the rhythmic *shush-shush* of his own heartbeat in his ears. Decian made a soft noise of enjoyment, the pleased hum resonating along Caius' nerves and sending a wave of gooseflesh across his skin.

Decian stoked the fire of his pleasure with slow deliberation, neither teasing nor hurrying. Time lost meaning, until Caius felt his approaching climax begin to coil, hot and insistent at the base of his spine. He steeled himself, sliding his fingers to cup Decian's jaw and guide him up and away. The younger man looked at him with a question in his eyes—lips wet and swollen, cheeks flushed beneath his dusky complexion... a slight furrow forming between his brows.

"Let me finish you," he said.

Caius urged him upright. "Come up here and let me finish both of us," he retorted.

He guided Decian to straddle his thighs, sitting high enough that their hips pressed together and the younger man's weight rested well above the bandages covering his crossbow injury.

"Your wound—" Decian began.

"Is fine," Caius insisted. A lie, though not a very large one—the pressure of Decian straddling his leg did cause him a bit of pain, but it also worked to pull him back from the edge of release long enough for him to accomplish his goal.

Between them, they got Decian's breeches and smallclothes open. His cock sprang free, hard and leaking at the tip. Caius made a low noise of appreciation and hitched Decian forward another fraction so their lengths slid against each other— swordplay of an altogether enjoyable kind. Caius spit into his right hand and gathered their shafts together in his grip, jerking them slowly at first, then faster.

Decian groaned, bracing one hand on Caius' good shoulder and the other against the fallen tree trunk. His hips flexed in time with Caius' stroking, and he curled forward a bit awkwardly until he could catch Caius' lips in a kiss every bit as sweet as the one that had started all this.

It wasn't long until Decian shuddered and spilled, coating Caius' hand and smoothing his grip to something warm and liquid. The pleasure that had been lurking beneath Caius' skin gathered into a tight knot and held... held... growing and heating until it finally broke free in a warm rush. The kiss had grown sloppy as Decian lost control, but Caius curled into it regardless as his seed pulsed and spurted between them.

They breathed against each other's lips, panting as their muscles uncoiled into sated languor. Decian slid halfway off his body, leaning against Caius' uninjured side with their legs still tangled together.

"You're very good at that, you know," he said.

"So are you," Caius managed.

Decian waved one hand in a vague, uncoordinated gesture. "There wasn't much to do in prison. One of my cellmates loved sucking cock. He was a bit of an arse most of the time, really. But it was... educational, I guess?"

Caius wasn't sure what to say to that, so he made a noncommittal noise and settled Decian closer against him. They lay together for some considerable time, boneless in the midday warmth. Somehow, this part was both new and painfully old in its familiarity.

In the military, occasional relations among the men were tacitly accepted, but they were generally pragmatic affairs not laden with emotion. Two men agreed to get each other off, after which they parted and went about their business. But this... casual warmth, this shared moment of post-coital vulnerability—it reminded him of lying curled together in bed with Serah after their lovemaking. And that realization frightened Caius more than battles, or treason, or assassins with crossbows in the woods.

"I should wet a cloth in the stream so we can clean up," Decian mumbled, making no move to actually get up and do so.

"For what it's worth, I think my clothing took the brunt this time," Caius said, with an equal lack of ambition to move. Perhaps it was a function of age and experience—or mere jadedness—but Caius couldn't raise much worry over the prospect of a random person in the street examining his crotch for evidence of dried spunk during the ride home. In the end, most people didn't pay that much attention to their surroundings.

Decian craned down to look at his breeches. "Huh. So it did."

They lay together for a bit longer, until one of the hounds wandered up and sniffed at Caius' face. He waved it off, trying not to think about the fact that the same dog had probably been picking bits of Jona out of its teeth not so long ago.

"I suppose we should get back," Decian said with clear reluctance.

Caius made a vaguely affirmative noise, surprised by the sense of loss he felt when Decian untangled their legs and levered himself upright. He put his clothing to rights, then went to rummage in his saddlebags, retrieving a rag and dipping it in the stream. He offered the damp cloth to Caius, who took it and made a half-hearted effort to clean himself up. When he'd tucked himself away and done up his undergarments and breeches, he accepted a hand up from Decian. They brushed grass and bits of bark off each other, and

Decian brought Caius' horse to stand next to the downed log for mounting.

With Decian holding the gelding's head to steady him, Caius was able to clamber aboard without too much trouble. Decian gathered up the remains of their meal and got on the pony, whistling to the dogs to call them to heel.

The ride back to the palace was uneventful, but Caius couldn't escape a sense of melancholy. This was stolen time, he knew. Things wouldn't always be this easy, and he was asking for future strife by not resisting his attraction to Decian more strongly. This was not a world in which an imperial legatus and a palace houndsman could dally their days away curled together in the woods, with no one being the wiser.

He needed to stop this foolishness and convince Decian to leave before disaster struck. But when they arrived at his house after returning the dogs to the kennel, instead of saying '*You shouldn't spend time with me anymore,*' he found himself saying, "Come with me to the gymnaestra tomorrow."

Decian gave him a curious look. "You're going to a gymnaestra with your leg only half healed? Is that a good idea?"

"It's for my shoulder, not my leg," he explained. "It gets worse when I don't work it regularly."

The pleased, slightly crooked smile that Caius was beginning to crave like a drug lit Decian's face. "Then I'd enjoy that a great deal. I can have your horse here about the same time as today."

Caius nodded. "Until then."

He watched as Decian took up the gray gelding's reins and rode off on his pony, heading for the royal stables. He told himself that the gymnaestra would be a good place to speak to Decian at length about the wisdom of leaving Amarius... and knew it was a lie.

FOURTEEN

That evening, Caius sent a message to the palace to inform them that he would be returning to duty in two days. Briefly, he entertained the fantasy of leaving Amarius with Decian and moving to some idyllic and doubtless fictional rural paradise. Perhaps they could return to the village of his youth. Upon his mother's death a few years ago, he had technically inherited the land that his parents had lived on—though in his absence it had probably been taken over by squatters.

One way or another, they could find a place somewhere—raise horses and hounds while pretending to be nothing more than business partners running a venture together.

He scoffed. *Yes.* And then the locals could run them out of town with pitchforks and torches after catching them in some indiscretion—either before or after the empire tore itself apart from the inside out during a fight over the royal succession.

He was a fool. Worse, he was quickly becoming an *old* fool, bewitched by a beautiful younger man who only looked twice at him out of gratitude for Caius having spared his life.

Morning rolled around, and Decian arrived as promised to accept Caius' ill-conceived invitation to the gymnaestra. He decided to allow himself this last day of self-indulgence. At the end of it, he would lay out his concerns and try one more time to convince Decian to leave the city. After that, the decision would be up to him. Caius would put distance between them, and if Decian still insisted on staying in Amarius, no doubt some younger, more charming companion would eventually catch his eye.

Caius hadn't thought to ask if Decian was inclined toward women as well as men. In the end, he supposed it wasn't really his business. Best-case scenario, Decian would end up somewhere far away with a sweet wife who loved him, living in safety and obscurity. Caius would do everything he could to make that happen.

"Have you ever visited a gymnaestra before?" he asked, not wishing to make assumptions.

"Never," Decian said. "The town where I grew up with my mother wasn't far from Amarius, but it was small. We didn't come into the city."

Caius wondered what had become of the emperor's Kulawi mistress after her son was thrown into prison at the age of sixteen, but it seemed insensitive to ask. He doubted the story had a happy ending.

He focused on the practical instead. "This one has a combination of areas set aside for athletic training, along with public baths," he explained. "Only men are allowed. Most will be naked. It's a more relaxed atmosphere than most in the capital, but discretion is still necessary."

Decian shot him an amused glance. "Are you worried I'll proposition someone?"

Caius flushed, realizing how his words had probably sounded.

His companion gave him an assessing look. "The prospect of being outed as an invert really worries you, doesn't it?"

Caius hesitated, framing his answer carefully. "I'm an advisor to the imperial family — in name, at least," he said. "If such a scandal were to come out, it wouldn't go well for me... but it would go far worse for you."

The corner of Decian's mouth quirked up, but it wasn't an expression of humor. "Yes," he said lightly. "I mean — heavens above — they might even decide to execute me or something."

Caius winced.

"On a related note," Decian went on, "if I'm going to be parading around in this gymnaestra with my bits on display, is anyone going to make a fuss about the state of my back? I've never seen it directly, but I imagine it's not a suitable view for polite company."

Caius shook his head. "No, you don't need to worry about that. It's not that sort of gymnaestra."

Indeed, the gymnaestra at the corner of Vaia Condora and the Pradi Imeno wasn't frequented by nobles and courtiers. It was a haven for old soldiers, former gladiators, and other rough characters who lived and died by the strength of their muscles. That was why Caius came here. People rarely asked questions beyond superficial small talk, and seldom offered opinions on anything of substance. They came, they took exercise, they made use of the bathing facilities and rubdowns. Then they left, and didn't spare much thought for any of their fellow members.

Caius led the way to a line of hitching posts. They tied the horses securely next to a trough filled with fresh water and went inside. The building, while large, wasn't grand. The man watching the door nodded at Caius in recognition and waved them through, not commenting on Caius' obvious limp. Inside, the sound of weights clanging and the occasional grunt of effort echoed off the tiled walls.

"Changing room's over here," Caius said, gesturing Decian inside. At this time of day, the place wasn't well attended. Nevertheless, a gray haired man looked up from one of the bench seats where he was lacing up his boots.

"Caius!" he exclaimed. "Don't normally see you here so early. Bringing a new friend, I see?"

"Hello, Olivio," Caius said. "An acquaintance, yes. This is Decian. I thought he might appreciate this place."

Olivio gave Decian a thorough onceover. "Fellow soldier, are you?"

Decian offered him a pleasant smile and shook his head. "No, nothing like that—I'm far too headstrong. Even if they'd let me join in the first place, I'd have been drummed out in fairly short order, I expect."

Olivio laughed. "At least you're honest about it. Well, I'm off home to the missus. Make sure old Caius here doesn't overdo it after whatever the hell he did to his leg."

"I'll try," Decian agreed.

After he left, Caius showed Decian where he could stow his clothing and belongings. Some gymnaestra had fancy padlocked compartments in the changing rooms to discourage theft. The Condora gymnaestra engendered a strong sense of brotherhood among its members. That, combined with an owner who made it known that anyone caught stealing in his establishment would be hunted down and murdered in his bed — *slowly* — meant that problems with theft were rare.

After they'd both disrobed, Caius led the way to the main exercise chamber and its attached courtyard. Decian looked around the place with fascination, taking in the grizzled men sparring with heavy leather punching bags, lifting and lowering spherical metal weights with handles, and engaging in bodyweight exercises.

They were a motley bunch. One might almost say disreputable. The fact that Caius was more comfortable here than in the echoing marble halls of the palace neatly described the state of his life these days.

He saw Decian's eyes light up, his attention falling on the circle laid out for wrestling. In it, two men close to his age were grappling, hands clutching and slipping against oiled skin.

"Seen something that interests you, I take it? Go on, then," Caius said. "I'll be over by the weights. Don't do anything I wouldn't do."

Decian shot him a knowing smirk, and Caius cursed himself silently. *Damn it*, he was supposed to be talking Decian into leaving Amarius... not lobbing double entendres at him.

"We both know that's not much of an admonition," Decian pointed out, and left to investigate the wrestlers.

Once he was out of hearing range, Caius sighed gustily and went to claim a bench and a weighted ball. Because he apparently enjoyed torturing himself almost as much as he enjoyed sabotaging himself, he sat down so he had a clear view of the wrestling circle. His left shoulder was a mess after so many days of complete inactivity. He began the familiar, painful process of forcing the damaged muscles into use—first by stretching, and then by lifting the weight, circling his arm through its limited range of motion.

Decian quickly fell into conversation with the two men who'd been grappling. Inevitably, before long he was oiling himself up, laughing at something one of the others had said. The clear noise carried over the sounds of men at exercise, trapping Caius' attention almost as much as the sight of his long, lean muscles glistening tawny in the light.

He was good, too. Caius might have expected him to be competent at brawling after years spent in prison, but this clearly wasn't the first time he'd wrestled in the classical style. Caius watched, rapt, as Decian held his own against his more experienced opponent by means of sheer strength and flexibility.

"He's a tough one. Where'd you find him, anyway?"

Caius blinked, startled, as the man who'd addressed him sat down on the end of his bench.

He was a familiar face in the gymnaestra, but Caius didn't have a name to put to the face. More importantly, he didn't have a prepared answer to the question.

Good god above… what had happened to him over the past few years? He'd commanded troops during wartime, for fuck's sake — devised military strategy, won major battles against seasoned opponents. Now he floundered for words after being caught staring at a younger man engaged in a wresting clinch.

"On the wrong end of trouble," he managed after a brief hesitation.

The man laughed. "That I can believe. You're the legatus, aren't you? The one from the palace?" He gestured at Caius' bandaged leg. "Looks like you and trouble have been spending too much time together lately."

Something about the fellow's interest prickled at his instincts, but Caius only shrugged. "I don't go looking for it," he said. "But there's not much I can do when it comes knocking on my door."

Liar, said the little voice that lived in the back of his head.

With his shoulder aching and his thoughts oddly disturbed after the brief exchange, he excused himself and returned the weight to its shelf. Decian was still with the pair of wrestlers, and appeared to be getting instruction on a specific move. Suddenly unwilling to watch Decian's long limbs twining with his opponent's any longer, Caius excused himself and headed for the steam room. It was empty, and he took advantage of the opportunity to stew both physically and mentally. After a few minutes, the door opened and Decian joined him.

"There you are," he said. "How's the shoulder?"

"Hurts like hell, which means it will be easier to use tomorrow," Caius said gruffly. He steeled himself. "We need to talk about you leaving."

Decian settled back and looked at him, brow furrowing. "Do we? I thought we already talked about me leaving. I distinctly remember pointing out that I now have food, a place to sleep, and a job I rather enjoy doing for the first time in a decade." He paused. "Not to mention... the other benefits."

The other benefits need to stop, Caius wanted to say. He opened his mouth, even drew breath to utter the words—only to have them wither and die on his tongue.

"It's not safe," he said instead.

Decian's expression turned intent. "Life's not safe. I'm not sure that's a good enough reason to stop living it."

Caius stared at him... at the sweat and oil making his skin shine dark bronze. His eyes were guileless—without artifice, but full of conviction. Caius felt himself giving in to their magnetic pull, cursing his weakness all the way down. If he was enough of a fool, would he eventually be able to convince himself that succumbing to this temptation was some grand act of rebellion against society's injustice, rather than the base cowardice and selfishness he knew it to be?

"It will end badly," he said, not sure which of them he was warning.

"Then it ends badly," Decian replied simply. "In my experience, most things eventually do."

Caius held his gaze, unblinking. "That's a grimmer outlook than I've come to expect from you."

Decian didn't look away. "I said *most* things end badly. Not *all* things."

The little quiver of yearning that bloomed in Caius' chest as the words hit home hurt more than hopelessness ever had.

FIFTEEN

They lingered in the steam room for a little longer, then moved to the bathing room. An attendant poured water from an amphora over each of them to wash away the oil and sweat. Caius declined the cold pool—not wanting to submerge his leg wound until it was healed more fully—but Decian waded in and dunked beneath the surface to cool off.

Both of them skipped the warm pool. Returning to the changing room, they dressed and headed out to the street. A young man entered as they were leaving. He paused, his gaze landing on Caius and sticking there for longer than seemed appropriate. When the lad's attention moved to Decian, Caius felt his expression darkening into a scowl.

The lad noticed and flushed, jerking his eyes downward and squeezing past them to enter without a word. It was only as he disappeared inside that Caius recognized him as the young man from Saleene and Zuri's brothel—the one who'd offended the noblewoman somehow.

"Someone you know?" Decian asked curiously. He lifted an amused eyebrow. "Should I be jealous?"

Caius shook himself free of his moment of preoccupation. "He works at a brothel in this part of the city. I didn't expect to see him here, that's all."

"Ooh, now I'm *definitely* jealous," Decian teased, and Caius turned the scowl on him.

"Not like that," he said severely. "I think they must throw him at the occasional frustrated wife who comes in for relief."

Decian let out a bark of surprised laughter. "Oh, dear. Never mind, then." He glanced up to gauge the position of the midday sun. "So, what's next? How's your leg holding up?"

In a refreshing change of pace, his leg actually hurt less than his shoulder at that moment.

"It's all right," he said. "Do you need to get back to the kennels?"

Decian smiled and shook his head. "Not until mid-afternoon. As long as the dogs are all healthy and not needed for a hunt, it's mostly a matter of feeding and exercising them in the courtyard twice a day. Well—that and keeping everything clean. But Pip's the apprentice, so he gets stuck with most of the dirty jobs."

Caius snorted. "If he's still taking half your pay, I would certainly hope so."

"He's a good lad," Decian said. "Without him, I doubt I'd have been able to pull this off to the extent that I have. He's young, but if I do end up having to leave on short notice at some point, he should have the job... not someone else. The dogs trust him, and he's got a steady hand with them."

If Decian ended up having to leave against his will, Caius suspected that the dogs would be the least of their worries. Aloud, he only said, "I'll keep it in mind if it ever comes to that. Come on—if you don't have anywhere else to be just yet, let's go get a drink and a meal."

>⸺⚜⸺<

Choosing the Cock's Crow tavern for their meal was, perhaps, a mistake. At the very least, Caius supposed it meant that he'd capitulated to the inevitability of Decian staying in Amarius for now. The modest drinking den fronted Saleene's brothel—someplace Caius hadn't been since the evening after Decian had crashed into his life almost two weeks previously.

"I have to say," Decian observed as they entered through the main doors, "your tastes aren't what I would have expected."

Caius shot him a sidelong glance. "What would you have expected?"

"After seeing your house?" Decian gestured vaguely with one hand, as though trying to outline something grand. "I dunno. Rich places. White marble and mosaics everywhere. Pies made of hundreds of swallows' tongues and wine with flakes of gold floating in the goblets."

"Good god," Caius muttered. "It's bad enough that I have to make an appearance at those kind of functions a few times a year at the palace. Why on earth would you think I'd seek out that sort of ridiculous frippery during my time off?"

Decian let out a breathless laugh. "Well, consider me thoroughly disillusioned. Not to mention a bit relieved. For one thing, I have no idea if you're actually supposed to drink the gold flakes in the wine, or what."

A smile pulled at one side of Caius' mouth. "If you have to ask, you're generally not invited to those sorts of parties in the first place. In this tavern, however, if there are flakes of anything floating in your goblet, I would definitely advise against drinking them."

It was something of an exaggeration, honestly. While far from grand, the Cock's Crow served decent food and drink at a reasonable price. If the place had been horrible, Saleene wouldn't have set up shop above it... and Caius wouldn't frequent it.

Decian scoffed. "Oh, *please*. Hello — ten years in prison? I've swilled more weak wine with mysterious chunks floating in it than you've had hot dinners. And probably swilled more weak *vinegar* with chunks in it, as well."

It still struck Caius as surprising how little bitterness Decian seemed to harbor when it came to his years of unjust imprisonment. It would have been easy to let the quip ruin his mood, reminding him of the dark circumstances surrounding them. Instead, he forced himself to reply in kind, keeping things light. "If that's so, then you should already know the answer to your original question. Of course you drink the gold."

"And shit it out the next day?" Decian asked in disbelief. "Seems wasteful."

"I think that's probably the point," Caius mused.

He glanced around the establishment, looking for an empty table. Instead, his eyes landed on a familiar, distinctive pair of faces seated in the corner. Saleene caught his eye, raised her eyebrows in mild surprise, and jerked her chin in a brusque motion, beckoning him over. Beside her, Zuri — her dark-skinned partner — looked up curiously, following the direction of her gaze.

Caius weighed the possible pitfalls involved in introducing his new male lover to his favorite prostitute for only an instant before making a strategic decision. He glanced at Decian and indicated the table. "Over here. There's someone I'd like you to meet, if you're amenable."

Decian shrugged agreeably, giving the pair at the table a curious look.

There were hazards here, to be sure. For one thing, Caius had no idea how Decian was likely to react to Saleene... but Saleene could take care of herself in that regard. The cold, tactical part of him — the same part that had deserted him earlier — was working overtime now. If the meeting went smoothly, Saleene and Zuri could potentially act as a safe haven for Decian in the event that he had to run, at least for a night or two. Whether they'd be willing to do so was another question, of course — especially since Caius wasn't about to offer details of Decian's true identity as a condemned bastard son of Emperor Constanzus.

"Hullo, Saleene," he greeted, as he limped up to the table. "Hullo, Zuri. We just stopped by for a drink and a meal."

Zuri gestured at the empty chairs. "Join us, Legatus. Who's this?"

150

Decian beat him to the punch, dipping his head in a shallow bow of greeting. "I'm Decian. You're friends of Caius', I gather? It's a pleasure to meet you."

Saleene's smile was cool. "Business associates, more accurately. Pleased to meet you, Decian. Have a seat, both of you."

Caius pulled out a chair and lowered himself into it carefully, grimacing as his wound twinged. "Saleene and Zuri run the brothel upstairs. I met Decian recently, when he became the new master of hounds at the palace."

A wry smile wrinkled the corners of Decian's eyes. "Oh, yes. The legatus and I hit it off immediately. He's been showing me around the city."

Saleene smiled back, her incisive gray eyes taking them both in with a look of speculation. "Has he, indeed? Well, our dearest Caius *is* widely known for his geniality and convivial nature."

"Uh... he is?" Decian asked, giving her an odd look. He turned to Caius. "You've certainly been keeping *that* part quiet. You should have mentioned."

Zuri let out a short bark of laughter.

Caius took it in good humor, not offended by the teasing. "You always seem to have enough bonhomie for both of us, so I never felt it was worth the effort."

Saleene raised an eyebrow at the banter. "Goodness. If nothing else, you've certainly managed to lighten his mood since the last time I spoke to him, Decian. I'm impressed."

Zuri gestured toward Caius. "What happened to your leg, anyway?" she asked, fearlessly direct as always.

"I got between an assassin and his intended target," Caius replied.

"You got between *two* assassins and their intended target, you mean." Decian frowned. "Whoever that was supposed to be. Do you even know?"

"No idea," Caius said. "By the time I was in a position to ask, they were already dead. The imperial family, presumably."

Zuri raised a hand and beckoned a serving girl over. "Bring us some more wine, Fassa. And two more bowls of stew, please."

The girl nodded and hurried off to fetch their meal.

Saleene leaned back in her chair. "Hmm. Still leaping between Constanzus and danger, Caius? I'd have thought you'd had enough of that job after the first time."

Caius regarded her curiously, his brows drawing together. "I wasn't aware you even knew about that. It was a long time ago."

"People talk," Saleene told him. She flicked her fingers in a dismissive gesture. "But enough about our illustrious emperor. How did you come to work at the palace, Decian? I take it you're not originally from Amarius?"

"No, I grew up in a village some distance outside the city," Decian said. "Mostly, I was in the right place at the right time when the old master of hounds left the position."

"He has a way with the dogs. Far more so than the previous houndsman," Caius added, with a flash of inappropriately dark humor.

"What about you, Zuri?" Decian asked, neatly redirecting the conversation. "You're Kulawi, aren't you? That's where my mother came from, you know."

"That's right," Zuri said, easily enough. "I arrived here with my father on an extended trade mission when I was young. Grew up here, really— so when he left to return to our village, I decided to stay behind."

Her dark eyes flicked to Saleene, glowing with a look of affection that hinted at the real reason she'd stayed. Caius had noted the obvious devotion between the pair on many occasions over the years. He didn't claim to understand how their relationship worked when both of them slept with random men for money, but there was little question that somehow, it did.

Decian nodded, shifting his attention to Saleene. "And what about you? You're... cross-spirit, is that right? That's what my mother used to call it, I think. A woman born into a man's body?"

It was direct to the brink of rudeness, but Decian's tone made it clear he wasn't judging, just curious.

Saleene—who'd doubtless heard far more insulting descriptions on too many occasions to count—replied with good grace. "Yes, that's what Zuri calls it, too. When I was younger and living as a man, I was a soldier in a rebel army across the border in Utrea. I was captured during a skirmish with Alyrion forces and brought to Amarius as a slave."

"The businessman who bought her owned a string of brothels in the city," Zuri went on. "She was good with numbers and accounting, so after a few months, he put her in charge of several of them."

Saleene shrugged. "Like you, Decian, I had a natural affinity for the work. I eventually earned my freedom and bought my own brothel. Now I can live as I choose."

"That's important," Decian said. "Sometimes I think it might be the most important thing of all."

The wine and food came as he was speaking, and once it was settled in front of them, Zuri lifted her goblet. "I'll drink to that," she said.

SIXTEEN

They all raised their drinks, tapping the rims together in solidarity. Caius looked around the table, wondering how he could feel envious of a pair of prostitutes and an escaped prisoner when he lived in an extravagant house and rubbed shoulders with the nobility.

Now I can live as I choose, Saleene had said. And that was the thing, wasn't it?

Could Caius choose something different? Again, the ridiculous vision of a quiet smallholding in the country slid across his thoughts—some magical, fantastical place where politics didn't exist and no one cared who he bedded. Again, the vision of Alyrios crumbling to dust beneath his feet followed close on its heels.

He blinked the moment of self-indulgence away and began to eat. The conversation slowed as they shifted their focus to the food.

"Oh—by the way," Caius said into the lull, "we ran into your troublesome pretty boy at the Condora gymnaestra this morning. It surprised me—he doesn't really seem the type."

"Pretty boys need to keep their pretty physiques," Zuri said around a mouthful of stew.

Caius considered pointing out that his particular gymnaestra didn't tend to cater to boys, much less pretty ones... but the subject was unimportant. It had been a minor coincidence, nothing more.

Outside, the sound of an angry, chanting crowd cut through the buzz of conversation in the tavern, growing loud enough that Decian craned around to look toward the door with a frown.

"What's that about?" he asked.

"Protesters," Saleene replied in a level tone. "There are more on the streets every day."

"A mob nearly burned down the temple on Vaia Sacrii last night," Zuri added. "Did you hear about it?"

"*What*?" Caius said, and unpleasant jolt of surprise hitting him in the chest. The Temple of Deimok on Vaia Sacrii was one of the largest churches in the capital. The idea that a pagan mob would dare attack it spoke of a level of unrest far beyond anything Caius would have predicted.

"I did tell you that change was coming—and that it wouldn't be gentle," Saleene reminded him dryly.

Decian looked between them. "Why do I feel like I'm missing something here? What exactly are the protesters protesting?"

Both Zuri and Saleene shot him odd looks.

"You don't know? How long did you say you'd been in Amarius?" Zuri asked.

"Not long enough to get embroiled in this morass," Caius answered for him.

"The Church is convening an ecumenical council to discuss the fate of pagan practitioners who refuse to convert to Deimonism," Saleene said. "The pagans take exception to the fact that they're not even to be allowed a voice during the discussion."

Decian's expression settled into lines of distaste. "Oh. *Religion*. I'm sorry I asked."

Zuri stared at him. "People will die if the radical wing of the Church gets its way."

"People *always* die when they start arguing about whose god is better," Decian retorted.

Caius was still struck with unease over the idea that things in the capital had deteriorated to such a degree while he'd been sitting at home, nursing a wounded leg. "Burning down temples won't help their cause."

Saleene turned a hard expression his way. "I find it fascinating when people are more appalled by the idea of a building being burned by a mob than the idea of a person being burned at the stake by a judge."

"Is that what's going to happen?" Decian asked. "People being burned at the stake?"

"Not if the moderate voices inside the Council prevail," Caius said firmly. "Which would be a more likely outcome if the pagans would stop provoking them."

Outside, the volume of chanting reached a crescendo, then began to fade as the protesters passed them by and continued down the street.

"Pagan lives hang in the balance, their fate to be decided by a body that refuses to so much as hear their testimony or allow them to be present for the debate," Saleene pointed out. "How do you expect them to react?"

158

"I expect them to be angry and afraid," Caius shot back. "Which doesn't change the fact that by marching through the streets and openly attacking Deimonist temples, they increase the chances that the zealots within the Council will ultimately hold sway."

"And if that happens, hundreds will die at the hands of the Church, if not thousands," Saleene finished.

"Even if the worst happens, they could always just agree to convert," Caius said. "It's better than dying."

Saleene and Zuri's faces were unreadable, but Decian's quiet voice broke the silence. "My mother worships the old gods from her homeland. She has since she was a little girl. Her beliefs have always been important to her."

Caius turned to him, the twisting discomfort in his stomach that accompanied any discussion of the upcoming Amarian Council intensifying as the words hit home. Decian's mother was Kulawi. *Of course* she worshipped the Kulawi gods. Did Zuri worship them as well? Was that why Saleene appeared to hold such strong opinions on the matter?

"I'm sure many in the capital feel the same way," he said carefully, aware that he'd never personally understood the level of passion and stubbornness that religion seemed to bring out in others. "But if it came down to it, would you not prefer to see her convert rather than have her fall afoul of the Church and risk death?"

Decian frowned. "I'd rather see a world where people didn't talk about burning other people alive because they disagree on a point of theology."

"Yes. Wouldn't *that* be a lovely world?" The tone of Saleene's reply was deeply sardonic. "In fact… while we're at it, I can think of a few other things I'd like to change as well."

So can I, Caius thought, though he didn't voice the sentiment aloud.

"Is your mother still living in your old village?" he asked Decian, realizing even as the words left his mouth that Decian might not know the answer to the question. He'd been locked up. It was quite possible he hadn't seen or heard from his mother in more than a decade.

His mouth quirked down. "I expect she's returned to Kulawi by now," he said.

"Then she's safe," Caius told him firmly, "no matter what the Council decides."

Decian shrugged, still looking unhappy. "I suppose so."

Was Zuri safe, though? And what would happen if Decian casually invoked the pagan gods in front of the wrong person at the palace, as he was occasionally wont to do?

Unsurprisingly, the conversation fizzled after that, each of them retreating into their own thoughts. They finished their meal with only a desultory back-and-forth about trivial matters, though Saleene continued to cast assessing glances at Caius when she thought he wasn't paying attention. When his bowl was empty and his wine mostly drunk, she tilted her head, regarding him openly.

"Since you're here, might I have a quick word in private, Legatus?" she asked, pausing to give Decian a brief smile. "You don't mind, do you?"

Decian blinked at her, then seemed to shake himself free of his reverie. "No, of course not. Zuri, maybe you could tell me more about where you came from in Kulawi? My mother was from one of the river tribes…"

Zuri shrugged and nodded, launching into a tale of her home village in the land across the Southern Desert. Saleene rose and gestured toward one of the private rooms in the back, indicating Caius should follow her. They entered the dim area with its single large table dominating the central space, and she closed the door behind them.

He limped over and turned to face her, crossing his arms and hitching a hip against the heavy wooden table to take the weight off his leg. "What's this about, Saleene?" he asked, genuinely curious.

Their relationship had been a fairly lengthy one for a prostitute and client, spanning all but the first few months of the four years he'd spent in Amarius. However, that wasn't to say they were friends, exactly. Saleene was nothing if not businesslike, and Caius was generally ill suited to conviviality — as she herself had pointed out not long ago.

Saleene leaned back against the wall next to the door and crossed her arms as well, mirroring him. "Am I right in thinking that Decian is your foolish cause, Caius? Your act of treasonous justice from a couple of weeks ago?"

Damn, but the woman should never be underestimated.

"What would make you think such a thing?" he asked blandly.

"The fact that I'm not a fool, mostly." She lifted her chin, looking down her patrician nose at him. "You've bedded him as well, haven't you."

Caius let a hint of a smile curl one corner of his lips. He knew it didn't reach his eyes. "I'm not certain our business relationship entitles you to ask me questions like that."

She matched the smile. "It wasn't a question. And if you're bringing him around to the Cock to try to ingratiate him with me, I'd say that entitles me to some answers." She paused, her expression growing serious. "He seems lovely. He's been good for you, too. So... where does the 'treason' part come in?"

Caius sighed, capitulating. "I can't tell you that, Saleene. I don't even think *he* knows the details."

"You're trying to make contacts for him, aren't you? To give him options, if whatever game you're playing unexpectedly goes tits-up. Come on—give me something to work with here."

Caius hesitated. "He was a prisoner unfairly slated for execution. He escaped death—mostly by pure chance—and I helped him hide in plain sight rather than killing him myself... or turning him in."

"Execution? What was his crime?" Saleene asked, her tone neutral.

"Being born," Caius told her.

Silence settled over the room. Eventually, Saleene broke it.

"As I said, people talk," she said. "There have been mutterings about prisoners being brought to the palace for execution in recent weeks. Some say they're imperial bastards who've recently become... *inconvenient*."

Caius shook his head. "I'm sorry, but I truly can't say any more about it." He hesitated. "Well... maybe this much. He was thrown in with the palace hounds after the beasts had been starved for a week. That was supposed to be his method of execution — getting torn apart by ravenous dogs."

Her eyebrows shot up. "God's *balls*, Caius. And you somehow installed him as *master of hounds*? That's... a bit on the nose, don't you think?"

"It's a long story," he said, feeling suddenly, unutterably tired. "I'll concede that when I saw you and Zuri dining today, it occurred to me that the two of you might be useful acquaintances for Decian to make. But you'll have to take my word that it was an impetuous decision, not part of some grand, overarching strategy. I appear to have lost my facility for grand strategy quite thoroughly in the years since I left the battlefield."

She studied him, doubtless taking in the tired slump of his shoulders and the way he leaned against the table to coddle his injured leg. After the past two weeks, he felt every inch the used-up old warhorse that he was — lame, and overdue to be put out to pasture.

"Are you in love with him?" she asked.

He exhaled forcefully, taken by surprise. "In *love* with him? What the hell kind of question is that, Saleene?"

She didn't back down or break eye contact. "Oh, don't mind me—I'm just trying to figure out if I've lost a client permanently or not. That's not a complaint, by the way. Like I said before, it seems he's been good for you."

Caius gave a single, frustrated shake of the head. He turned away from her, in favor of examining the rough-plastered wall as though it were the most fascinating thing he'd ever seen. "Let's put it this way. When this situation inevitably comes crashing down around my ears, I'll pay you whatever you ask to bugger me so hard that I forget my own name for a week. Assuming my head is still attached to my shoulders and not severed by an executioner's axe, of course."

"You're still trying to play both ends against the middle, Caius," Saleene said. "Though I at least get the impression that you finally know which side you *should* be playing, now."

"I don't have a side, Saleene," he replied. "I'm fairly certain the side I want to play doesn't exist anymore."

"Caius, you absolute fool. You *do* have a side," she retorted. "He's sitting out there with Zuri as we speak."

To that, he had no reply.

Caius returned to the front room of the tavern to find Decian and Zuri chatting amiably. It was anyone's guess whether their tentative affinity would survive the full report Saleene was certain to give her partner as soon as they had privacy to speak.

Decian looked up at his approach with a smile. "Everything all right?"

"As much as it ever is," he replied.

"Right. Not a terribly reassuring reply, but whatever you say," Decian told him. "Are you ready to go? I should probably be getting back to the kennels soon, but I can drop you at your house and return your horse to the stables on my way."

"Yes, let's be going," Caius said. "Saleene... Zuri. Always a pleasure. Perhaps we can share a table again soon."

"Oooh, careful with the charm, Caius," Saleene warned. "Someone will mistake you for a gentleman."

Decian swallowed a laugh, and even Zuri cracked a smile.

"Fortunately, everyone at this table already knows me too well to make that particular mistake," Caius told them dryly. "Good afternoon, both of you."

They paid for their meal and left the tavern. Outside, Decian shot him a sidelong glance laced with humor. "I notice you didn't tell *them* not to do anything you wouldn't do."

"I wouldn't dare," Caius said.

The younger man seemed to have already forgotten their earlier, uncomfortable exchange about religion. Caius hadn't, though.

"I apologize if I was out of line earlier. I'm afraid I've always taken a practical approach to religion rather than a theological one."

"So I gathered," Decian said, though Caius could detect no anger in his tone. "Personally, I have very little use for any of it, even though I suppose some of what I grew up with must have stuck with me."

Caius only hoped the parts that had stuck with him didn't end up getting him in trouble.

"Still, it was thoughtless of me," he insisted. "I'm frustrated... with the Council, with the protesters... with all of it, I suppose. I watch events unfolding like two runaway wagons heading for a collision. And if any of the involved parties would simply step back for a moment and behave rationally, the disaster could be averted. But they won't. None of them will, and in the end, people will die. It only remains to be seen on how large a scale."

Decian nodded, thoughtful. "I've always been more concerned about the events immediately around me than with politics or religion... or any of the rest of it. I've had to stay focused on the here-and-now to survive. This is the first time I've really had a taste of the larger picture, and I can't say I envy you. Not one bit."

They reached the horses. Caius accepted a leg up, suppressing a pained grunt as he swung into the saddle and gathered up his gelding's reins.

"I suppose it's one thing when you have the kind of power that allows you to shape the larger picture to your liking," he said, as Decian untied the pony and scrambled onto its back. "But standing just outside the sphere of influence while watching everything go horribly wrong? Well, let's just say it grows old quickly."

They headed for the palace compound, winding through the back streets of Amarius. Caius couldn't help feeling on edge—watching their surroundings for any hint of trouble. Citizens went about their business. Wagons, riders, and people on foot crowded the roadways. The sound of clattering wheels and hooves against cobbles filled the air, along with the smell of people and animals, food and smoke and rotting garbage.

There was nothing out of the ordinary, although they did catch up to the crowd chanting anti-Church slogans at one point, riding parallel and a couple of blocks north of the marching protesters. Eventually, the mob turned onto a crossroad leading into a different part of the city, the sound of their voices gradually subsumed by the sounds of daily life.

When they'd successfully reentered the palace grounds and reached his house, Caius dismounted, looking at the familiar edifice with a combination of relief and dread. He had almost certainly pushed himself too hard today, before his wound was sufficiently healed. He knew on an intellectual level that he needed to rest, but he was also sick to death of staring at his own walls.

Decian leaned down and took the gelding's reins, ready to lead him back to the stables. He met Caius gaze and held it. "I could come back here tonight?" he offered. A sly smile slid across his face. "In case there's anything else you need help with, I mean."

The words *'that's not a good idea'* formed on the back of his tongue... but what came out was, "I'd like that." He frowned at himself, and quickly amended, "I'll be resuming my duties at the palace in the morning, though. After that, my time won't be my own. Not like it has been these past several days."

Decian only shrugged a shoulder. "I understand. Just try not to overdo it, all right? No more battling armed assassins until you've recovered from the last skirmish."

"I'll inform the assassins that they'll need to reschedule their dastardly plans to accommodate me," he said.

"You do that," Decian told him with a firm nod. "See you tonight, Legatus. Thanks for showing me around the city today." With a quick wink, he urged the pony around, leading the gelding alongside.

"Until then," Caius said to his retreating back, hating himself just a little bit more for his continuing weakness of will.

SEVENTEEN

When Caius entered his house, he was greeted by the sound of clattering pots and pans in the kitchen. Tertia poked her head out as he approached, giving him a brief head-to-toe inspection.

"You're looking better," she said. "Have you been out all day on that leg?"

"Since mid-morning," he told her. "I've already eaten, by the way."

"What, so you'll never need to eat again?" she asked. "Well, that *does* save me some trouble."

He huffed out an irritated breath and started past the kitchen, with the intention of returning to his room. After a few hitching steps, he paused and turned back. "Tell me something, Tertia. Would you say sympathies among the common people in Amarius lie more with the Church, or more with the pagans?"

She lifted her eyebrows in surprise, probably because he'd never asked her a question like that before. "About half and half, I'd say. Why?"

He shook his head, dismissing his own line of questioning. "Just a conversation I had with someone today in a tavern. Don't mind me—forget I asked."

"Minding you is my *actual job*, you dolt," Tertia said without heat. She took a breath as though to speak, but held it for a moment as she chose her words. "Outside of the imperial quarter, things are… complicated right now. Up until recently, I don't think most people gave a rat's testicles about what the pagans got up to—not until this Council nonsense came up, anyway. Now, everyone's got an opinion. The ones who were inclined to be worried are more worried, because there are pagans marching in the streets demanding rights. And the ones who were inclined to be sympathetic are more sympathetic, because they've got a better idea what's at stake now."

Caius took a moment to digest that, even though it basically confirmed his suspicions. "And what about you? What do you think?"

She straightened her spine, and Caius watched her walls going up before his eyes. "I'm just a lowly slave, *Legatus*. I don't discuss religion with my betters. I'm sure the emperor and his Council will decide what's best for all of us."

It was as clear a rebuke as if she'd told him to go straight to hell, and it brought the power imbalance between them into sharp relief. Caius was a respected general, seeking information about a matter important to the empire. Tertia was a slave who could be punished or even killed if she said the wrong thing to the wrong person.

"I understand," he said. "Thank you, Tertia. I'll retire to the garden for a bit while you finish what you were doing."

She scowled at him, as though fighting an internal debate. As he turned to leave, she said, "Most people in the palace don't look at things the same way as you, Legatus. You'd do well not to forget that."

He paused, not looking back at her. "Believe me," he told her, "there are days when I wish I *could* forget it."

Caius spent the rest of the afternoon and the first part of the evening turning the problem around and around in his head. The ideal outcome, as he saw it, would be for the moderate wing of the Church to prevail. Under their leadership, the pagans would be left more or less alone, in the belief that Deimok could sort them out as He saw fit after they died. As far as the moderate voices were concerned, the unbelievers would still end up suffering eternal torment for their wicked heresy — it would just happen a few years later than it otherwise might have.

Caius had no opinion on the disposition of souls after death, but he had some fairly strong opinions about rounding people up and setting fire to them because their neighbors claimed they were divining the future using chicken entrails or dancing under a full moon, or what have you.

There were genuinely dangerous pagan practitioners in the world, obviously. Caius had lost his father to one, and could easily have lost his life to another on the beaches of Eburos, during the botched invasion at Llanmeer. After what he'd seen during his forty-six years, if a shapeshifting pagan warlock ever found himself at the end of Caius' sword, Caius would run the fucker through without a second thought.

But that kind of real magic was vanishingly rare in Alyrios. The imperial family would have people believe that it had been wiped out generations ago—though Caius knew that to be a whole different kind of propaganda. It sure as hell hadn't been wiped out on Eburos. In addition, dragons had returned to the neighboring land of Utrea in recent years—and while the animals themselves might not be magical in the purest sense, the bonds their riders used to control them smacked heavily of witchcraft.

Caius hadn't heard of any shapeshifters infesting Alyrion lands in recent years. Not, in fact, since the one his father and the other guardsmen had killed at the cost of their own lives when he was a boy. That didn't mean none existed, but it certainly argued they weren't common. In the context of the current struggle, the term 'pagans' simply referred to people who still followed the old gods.

As long as they weren't hurting anybody, in Caius' view they didn't deserve a sentence of execution—no more than Decian deserved a sentence of execution for being born a bastard. But the pagans were angry. They were afraid for their lives, with good reason. And so they were making trouble, which only succeeded in fanning the flames of sentiment against them within the Council. That, in turn, fanned the flames of protest against the Council... and so the wheel turned.

Caius could see no practical way to break the cycle. Certainly, nothing that could be implemented by a single aging Legatus standing at the fringes of a ruling dynasty riddled with infighting.

The sound of someone entering through the front door broke him free from his thoughts. It had grown dark outside as he pondered the empire's troubles, the garden now illuminated only by the torches Tertia had lit before she left. They flickered in their sconces, casting a warm glow over Decian as he entered the open space. Humidity choked the air.

"You're going to get wet if you keep sitting there," said the younger man, by way of greeting. "There's a storm rolling in."

As if in response to his words, a gust of wind blew through the open area, whistling past the columns and rustling the leaves on the plants. Several of the torches blew out, and a fat raindrop splattered on the bench next to Caius' leg.

"Good thing you arrived in time to warn me," he said. "I might have drowned otherwise." He hauled himself to his feet as more raindrops followed. "I expect there's food in the kitchen. Hungry?"

"Always," Decian said, retreating under the cover of the hallway.

Caius followed him, joining him just as the skies opened. They were overdue for rain, and he enjoyed the sound of it overhead as he ushered Decian into the kitchen to investigate whatever food Tertia had left for him.

"Did your roof get repaired, I hope?" Decian asked wryly.

"As far as I know. At least, there was a fair amount of crashing and banging going on up there a few days ago."

"This ought to test the quality of their work, if nothing else," Decian said over the din of rain against baked ceramic tiles.

They put together plates of salted pork, pickled greens, and soft cheese, along with hunks of Tertia's ever-present bread — standing at the worktable to eat. The initial deluge eased into the pattering drumbeat of a steady shower, and by the time they were finished, it had slowed to a drizzle.

After hours spent brooding over a problem that couldn't be fixed, Caius resolved to set aside his worries until tomorrow, when he would once again be back in the vipers' den at the palace and unable to ignore the situation. Tonight, he was alone with a pleasant companion and nothing else to occupy him until morning.

"So," Decian began, affecting a long-suffering tone. "Have you thought of *anything at all* I could help you with, since I walked all the way out here and nearly got caught in a rainstorm?" His eyes dipped suggestively to a point below Caius' waist, before lifting again to meet his with a mischievous twinkle.

Caius let his lips twitch into a smile. "Well, for a start you can bar the front door so we can be certain we won't be interrupted."

"Why, Legatus—are you about to suggest something *scandalous*?" Decian asked. "I am *shocked*."

"I haven't even told you what I have in mind yet," Caius pointed out.

"True," Decian allowed. "But I'm certainly waiting with bated breath to find out."

He disappeared into the atrium and returned a few moments later, errand complete. Caius took a quick mental inventory—the back door would already be barred, and Tertia would have closed and secured all the shutters before she left. They were alone, their privacy bolstered further by the unpleasant weather outside. Nothing short of the death of the emperor himself would be likely to bring anyone to his residence in the dark and the rain.

He limped over to the shelves arrayed along one wall of the kitchen and ran his fingers over the array of bottles and jars stored there.

"Still hungry?" Decian teased.

Caius chose a glass vial of pure, uninfused oil and plucked it from the shelf. "Not exactly," he said. "Though I'm not averse to swallowing something else before the night is through. Tell me—have you ever fucked another man... or been fucked?"

Decian went still. "You mean penetrated?" He paused. "No, I..."

Caius turned to look at him, struck by the sudden hesitation.

Decian shook his head briskly, recalling himself from whatever thoughts had distracted him. "It happened sometimes in the prison. Not to me personally, although I did have to fight off other prisoners on a handful of occasions. It... uh... wasn't exactly the kind of thing you did for fun."

Realization struck, and Caius covered a wince. "*Ah.* Yes, I see what you mean." He paused, debating for a moment before continuing. "You're aware that some men take enjoyment from the act, when it's approached with proper care?"

Decian tilted his head. "You're one of those men, I take it?" His tone was more curious than wary.

Caius consciously relaxed his stance. "I am, yes. Which isn't to say I indulge all that often—and we needn't tonight, obviously. Not unless you're interested. If you are, I'm more than happy to receive, rather than giving. I enjoy both variations with the right partner."

Decian tilted his head, considering. After a moment, he shrugged. "Bring the oil, at least. I'll admit to being intrigued."

"Very well. Just don't expect me to oil myself up and wrestle you," Caius told him, remembering the way the younger man's skin had gleamed as he grappled with the pair in the gymnaestra. "You'd probably win, and my pride doesn't need the blow."

Decian snorted. "Another time, then. Maybe once your leg is healed."

Even with his bad shoulder to consider, it wasn't an altogether unappealing offer. "We'll see. Come on—even *I* draw the line at fucking in Tertia's kitchen."

EIGHTEEN

Caius turned and headed for his bedroom. Decian's surprised laughter followed him, making something in his chest grow lighter. Rain pelted them as they exited the interior hallway, slanting down beneath the overhang that ran around the edge of the garden. Caius led the way into his room and set the oil on the bedside table. He took a few moments to light several of the lamps hanging evenly spaced on the walls, wanting enough illumination for both of them to be able to see what they were doing.

Decian, by contrast, made straight for the feather mattress, flopping down on it with a groan of pleasure. "See, now... that's what I'm talking about. It's criminal that you don't properly appreciate this bed."

"Oh, I don't know about that. Its appeal is growing as we speak," Caius assured him, looking over his shoulder to enjoy the show as Decian wriggled around in search of the perfect position. He finished with the final lamp and turned. "Clothes off," he ordered, tugging at the lacing of his own shirt and shrugging it awkwardly over his bad shoulder.

While there was something to be said for slowly unwrapping a lover's layers, the truth was that their two previous encounters had both occurred with Decian more or less fully clothed. Caius had seen him bared, but only in the gymnaestra. Tonight, Caius wanted him naked while they were in a place where he could touch as well as look.

"Hmm," Decian mused, even as he toed off his boots. "Do I call you *sir* when you order me around like that?"

Caius barked out a laugh and started work on his trouser lacings. "*God*, no. You were right before—you'd make a horrible soldier. Which is not, I hasten to add, a criticism." He was able to get out of his own boots—albeit painfully—with the aid of the carved wooden boot-pull sitting on the floor in the corner. At that point, however, he was stymied... his leg having grown too stiff over the course of the day for easy removal of the rest of his clothing.

He sighed. "Well, this is embarrassing."

Decian had already shimmied out of his layers and tossed them onto the floor next to the bed. He looked up, intuiting the problem with a single glance. "Not to worry. I *did* ask earlier if there was anything I could help you with, after all."

He rolled off of the too-soft mattress and prowled toward Caius, stopping so close in front of him that a deep breath would have brushed their chests together. His hands skimmed down Caius' sides—catching his waistband, sliding the breeches over his hips and down. He crouched, unselfconscious in his nudity, and Caius' cock twitched with interest at the memory of those full lips wrapped around his length.

Decian helped him step out of his trousers, smallclothes, and stockings, throwing them carelessly aside once he was done. He stood in a single, smooth movement, his skin sliding against Caius' on the way up. A self-satisfied little grin crinkled the corners of his eyes, and Caius couldn't help but pull him in for a kiss.

Decian made a low noise of appreciation. Caius swallowed it greedily, winding his good arm behind Decian's back to pull their bodies flush from chest to knee. He felt the ropy scar tissue from the flogging where it crisscrossed the younger man's skin, but the unusual sensation was swallowed beneath the jolt of their cocks brushing together. Decian's hips flexed, rutting against Caius shamelessly. He was already hard, and Caius wasn't far behind.

Caius let him continue for a bit, not immune to the appeal of simple frotting. Eventually, though, he eased Decian back until he could meet his eyes in the lamplight.

"Come on. Let's adjourn to that bed you're so fond of," he said. "You can put that oil to good use, if you're still interested."

Decian regarded him intently for a long moment before replying. "Actually, I think you should put it to good use on me, instead. You've got me curious now." He gave a small half-shrug. "If you like it enough to ask for it, then there must be something to it, right? I trust you."

Perhaps those three simple words shouldn't have affected him so, but Caius couldn't deny the sudden catch in his throat. He thrust the sentimental reaction aside, determined to ensure that Decian reaped generous rewards for his trust.

"As you like," he said. "There's often a small amount of discomfort involved at first... but if you decide at any point that it's not to your taste—"

"I'll let you know," Decian said with an easy smile.

Caius nodded. "It also requires the answer to an awkward question or two. Have you relieved yourself recently?"

Decian snorted. "Shortly before I came here. You're right, that is awkward."

"Not nearly as much as the alternative would be," Caius replied wryly, and Decian laughed outright. Caius decided there and then that he would never grow tired of hearing the sound of his laughter.

"Ever the practical military man," Decian teased, amusement still lurking in his tone. "Go on, then. How do you want me?"

Any way I can have you, Caius thought. He gestured to the bed. "Lie on your back. Get comfortable—we're going to be here awhile."

While Decian did so, he found a shallow bowl and poured a generous measure of oil into it. He arranged himself at Decian's hip and set the bowl within easy reach before leaning down to resume their earlier kiss.

If there was one advantage age had granted him, it was patience. He lavished attention on Decian's lips until the other man was panting against him, before moving to tease his nipples into taut brown points. Those, he plucked and tortured until Decian was writhing on the bed. Eventually, Decian reached for his own cock—pushed past his limits of self-control, though Caius had barely started on him.

"No," Caius said, grasping the wandering hand and placing it back on the bed.

Decian let out a frustrated groan. "This isn't at all what I'd pictured, just so we're clear," he said unsteadily.

"I know it's not," Caius told him, unrepentant, and went back to pinching and tugging the closest nipple. "Trust me."

Only when Decian stopped writhing, lying still except for the occasional full-body tremor, did Caius move lower. Decian's cock was a thing of beauty, hard and twitching—already leaking little dribbles of seed onto his flat stomach. Caius ran his finger lightly up its length from base to tip, gratified when the feathery touch drew a strangled noise and another pulse of pearly white.

He dipped his fingers into the oil—pleased that this, at least, was something he could still do left-handed—and cupped Decian's balls, kneading and tugging them lightly.

"F-*fuck*!" Decian stammered, thrusting up helplessly against nothing.

Caius let his fingers explore further, teasing sensitive skin until Decian's legs fell open of their own accord. More oil, and he slid down the final inch, brushing over the pucker he found there. Decian stilled as though suddenly unsure.

Caius met his eyes, sliding a single finger in slow circles around his tight rim. "All right?"

182

His companion's attention turned inward. He was silent for several moments before he nodded. "Yes. Don't stop."

Rather than reply with words, Caius leaned down awkwardly until he could kiss the tip of Decian's cock, which had softened a bit from its earlier ardor. Decian let out a sharp breath, his hips twitching. Caius indulged him with a long, slow suck of the head, licking the clinging drops of bitter saltiness clean. The pucker beneath his finger fluttered, and his fingertip sunk in a fraction, coming up against a second barrier of resistance.

Decian gasped.

Caius continued describing small, circular motions until Decian's last line of defense fell, allowing him inside. For several moments, he rested there without moving, sucking and laving Decian's cock until his body relaxed.

"That's... a decidedly odd sensation," Decian said, when Caius released his cock and started carefully stroking his way deeper.

"It is," Caius agreed. "Though it does get better."

Unhurried, he continued to tease Decian open until he was buried to the third knuckle. He was out of practice at the next part—it took a couple of attempts at curling his finger in a beckoning motion before Decian stiffened and arched, his hard prick jumping.

"*What* was that?" Decian demanded in an unsteady tone.

Caius smiled a predator's smile. "Oh, you mean this?" He curled his finger again, drawing an undignified noise from his partner. "Didn't I tell you it got better?" With that, he turned his attention to the highly enjoyable task of taking Decian to pieces without a single touch to his cock.

In the end, it took perhaps half an hour, three fingers, and roughly a third of the oil from the bowl to wring the first climax from him. He arched like a bow, his stomach muscles jerking as he stifled a cry. Caius' cock throbbed and twitched in sympathy as seed dribbled from the slit of Decian's prick, but did not spurt.

When he'd wrung as much as he could from his companion, he slid his fingers carefully free. Decian shuddered and went limp.

"Holy gods," he breathed. "That was... that was..."

Caius smirked down at him and rubbed an oily hand over his hard length, slicking himself thoroughly. "Oh, dear," he teased. "Did I somehow give the impression that we were done?"

Rain drummed against the roof over their heads. Decian blinked up at him, dazed and open and stunningly lovely in the warm, flickering light. "You're going to kill me, aren't you? I'm going to expire right here on this bed and sing your praises with my dying breath."

"Don't be ridiculous," Caius told him, rising from the bed on aching legs. Ignoring his nagging injuries, he manhandled Decian's unresisting body around until his hips rested at the edge of the mattress. "I've gone to far too much trouble to keep you alive."

Decian's head flopped back as Caius positioned himself between his legs, hooking his right elbow under Decian's left knee to tilt his hips up a bit. He lined himself up, nudging against Decian's entrance with steady pressure.

"Bear down for me, Decian," he ordered gently. "I promise to make it worth your while."

Decian groaned and did as he was told. Caius held his breath as his tip slid inside impossibly tight, silky heat. He froze, resisting the urge to thrust deep — instead waiting for Decian's body to adjust to him. Decian, too, was holding his breath. After a few seconds, his lungs emptied on a gusty sigh, and he wriggled his hips in Caius' grip. Caius slid a little deeper, and both of them gasped.

Caius worked into him by fractions, taking his time until he was fully seated. Beads of sweat had broken out on Decian's chest. "Move," Decian demanded. "Before I go mad."

He moved — cautiously at first. Decian flexed his hips, trying to meet him. Caius changed the angle, seeking, until he was rewarded with Decian's full-body shudder.

"There we go," he said. The heat and pressure was indescribable, demanding he seek more of it — deeper, faster. He refused to give into the urge; not until he'd wrung a second release from his lover.

There was a reason he'd avoided Decian's cock earlier, but now it was time. He freed the hand that wasn't supporting Decian's knee. Decian's other leg wrapped around his waist, pulling him in... keeping him close. Caius' fingers closed around Decian's cock, still hard despite his earlier climax.

Decian keened, his hands scrabbling against the bedclothes for purchase as Caius worked him steadily, in time with the shallow thrusts that were driving both of them toward climax.

Decian broke first, his muscles clenching hard as his spine arched. His seed spurted from his pulsing cock in thick ropes, painting his chest and belly. His passage clamped around Caius like a warm vise, pulling his release from him in waves of rippling pleasure. Caius breathed through it, savoring every second. Eventually, with Decian growing lax beneath him, he slid out. Both of them flinched at the loss, and Decian made a small, discontented noise that went straight to Caius' heart.

"Shh," Caius soothed, ignoring his unsteady legs long enough to help Decian sprawl full length onto the bed. "I'll get a cloth to clean us up and be right back."

He did so, aware that he'd pushed his body too hard today and not regretting it one bit. When he'd completed at least a cursory attempt to prevent them from becoming glued together by drying spunk as the night progressed, he set the cloth aside and climbed stiffly into bed, arranging the covers over them both.

Decian made a noise of happiness, sprawling along Caius' right side with his head resting on Caius' shoulder and a leg hooked possessively over his. Tawny, work-roughened fingers drew abstract patterns across Caius' chest, raising a pleasant shiver of gooseflesh in their wake. It had been... too long since Caius had something like this. So very, *very* long. Every circling thought in his mind was quieted; every physical ache and twinge buried beneath the warm, woolen blanket of affection and sexual lassitude.

He curled his good right arm around until he could stroke Decian's temple, fingertips caressing soft skin still dampened by cooling sweat. Decian's muscles — already lax with afterglow — melted completely against him. His wandering fingers stilled against Caius' chest, his palm coming to rest warm and heavy over Caius' heart.

"Mmm," Decian breathed, as Caius continued to stroke his temple and cheek. Above them, a new burst of rain pelted the tile roof. Wind whistled past the closed shutters, and a huff of soft laughter fluttered Decian's ribcage. He craned his neck to look up at Caius in the low lamplight. "You know — somewhere out there, an incompetent cutpurse is getting soaked to the skin right now. Serves him right, too."

Caius gazed down at him in mild confusion, trying to pull his wits together enough to decipher the statement. "A cutpurse? What do you mean?"

Decian lifted his hand, waving it vaguely in a 'doesn't matter' gesture before letting it fall back to rest on Caius' sternum. "It's not important. A man tried to follow me when I was on my way here earlier. A thief, I reckon. As soon as I noticed him, I doubled around to the stables and lost him." He yawned. "Anyway, he would have been disappointed. I've got nothing to steal. Not that I was carrying with me, at least."

A chill swept down Caius' spine, washing away his lethargy as effectively as if he'd stepped into the garden to stand under the downpour. He sat up, ignoring Decian's sleepy noise of protest.

"You were *followed*?" he demanded. "From the kennels? Describe this man to me. Decian—tell me *every single thing* you can remember."

NINETEEN

Decian rolled onto an elbow, a frown furrowing his brow. "Describe him? There's nothing much to describe. He was average looking. Dark clothing—nothing fancy. Why does it matter? There must be hundreds of petty thieves in a city this size."

"Did he follow you all the way from the kennels?" Caius asked urgently. "Was he armed?"

Decian blinked at him in the lamplight, clearly having no idea what had upset him so badly. "I mean... I wouldn't have thought so. I didn't notice him until I was about halfway here, anyway. And I didn't exactly stick around to see if he was armed."

Caius felt his pulse throbbing in his temple. Dread pooled in his stomach. "This is bad. Don't you *see*? Someone suspects you. You need to leave."

"What?" Decian shook his head sharply, as though to clear it. "Wait. Back up for a minute. Why would you assume this was anything more sinister than someone after a few coins?"

"*Think*, Decian!" Caius said. "We are *inside the palace compound*. There are no cutpurses roaming the emperor's grounds."

"This place is like a city inside a city," Decian protested.

"A *city* with high walls surrounding it and guards on every gate, day and night," Caius said grimly. "Guards who don't let anyone in or out unless they either know them personally, or they're carrying signed papers granting passage."

"That's..." Decian began, only to cut himself off. "So, you're saying someone was... what? Sent to follow me specifically?"

"Yes," Caius said, the chill of dread spreading from his stomach to his heart. "Someone is suspicious enough to want to know more about your comings and goings."

"And I led him here," Decian said slowly. "Well... I mean, I don't think I actually *did* lead him here. I stopped in and talked to the stable lads for a bit, and then snuck out the back to come the rest of the way to your house. I didn't see any sign of someone following me after that."

It was something, Caius supposed. But in the end, it wasn't where Decian had led his pursuer that was the issue. It was the fact that he was being shadowed in the first place.

"It doesn't matter," Caius said. "It's no secret that you've been spending half your time here since I was injured. The fact that you came here again tonight wouldn't gain them any new information. Though, normally I'd tell you to leave before it got any later, because seeing you slink out in the morning like a thief *would* give them information they could use against both of us."

The rain increased in intensity, battering against the roof.

"But tonight," Decian said slowly, "It would look stranger if you threw me out in the rainstorm, instead of letting me stay in one of your fancy guest rooms until the weather cleared."

"Just so," Caius agreed. He scrubbed his right hand through his close-shorn hair, thinking hard. "This isn't a game anymore—we have to get you out of the city. It was one thing when no one suspected you. But if someone is willing to make the effort to have your movements tracked inside the palace grounds—"

"They must know I'm not who I'm pretending to be." Decian looked as though his entire life had just been pulled from beneath him.

Which, of course, it had been.

It was a life crafted in the space of a mere couple of weeks... but for someone who'd been hauled off to prison at the age of sixteen, it was almost certainly the best life he'd known since childhood. Caius ached for him... or perhaps he ached for himself, selfishly, at the prospect of Decian being gone from his life. More likely, it was both, he decided.

He closed his eyes and took in a steadying breath. "Leave early in the morning and go back to the kennels. Act as though nothing is wrong. Don't breathe a word of this, not even to Pip. I'll beg off early tomorrow at Court—claim my wound is still paining me, or some such. Come here in the evening, just as you did tonight, but bring horses with you. If anyone asks, tell them you're taking me into the city to drink. If anyone follows you here, don't try to throw them off your trail. Don't let on that you've noticed them at all."

Decian frowned, still looking as though he'd been gut-punched. "What? Why not?"

"I don't want them on their guard. If we're followed beyond the palace gates, we'll lose them in the backstreets of the city. I'll take you to the port; buy you passage down the coast on the kind of ship where they ask no questions. I'll give you what money I can—enough to establish yourself somewhere far away from here." His chest tightened around the words, but he held his voice steady by force of will.

The expression on Decian's face gutted him.

"I don't want to leave," Decian whispered.

Caius lifted a hand, cupping the side of his face. "I don't want you to die," he said.

Decian's eyes slid closed. After an endless moment, he nodded.

"So. This is our last night, then." His voice sounded distant.

Caius swallowed. "It has to be. I'm sorry."

Decian leaned forward, his hand coming around the nape of Caius' neck. He pressed their lips together, and Caius squeezed his eyes shut at the desperate intensity of the kiss. He returned it as best he could, still cradling Decian's cheek in his palm, trying to convey not only his regrets, but also his gratitude for the gift of companionship Decian had given him.

After what might have been minutes or hours, Decian lowered his head to rest in the crook of Caius' shoulder. Throat aching, Caius wrapped his good arm around Decian's scarred back and held him tightly.

The door was barred. The shutters were closed. Even if Decian's shadow had decided to stand around in the rain for hours in hopes of catching a glimpse of his target, there was nothing for him to see from a vantage point outside the house. Caius would not force Decian into a guest room for appearances' sake. Not on their first and only night together. He eased the younger man down to lie with him on the bed as they had been before, and resumed his slow stroking of Decian's temple once they were settled.

Whereas the younger man had been sprawled across him in total relaxation before, now, he was clinging. Caius rested his chin on top of Decian's head, trying to ignore the heavy weight of grief settling across his shoulders with the familiarity of an old, tattered cloak. He couldn't give in to melancholia. Not yet, when he still had to get Decian away to safety. Right now, helping Decian escape Amarius was his only goal... the only important thing in his world.

The night grew deeper, the rain continuing off and on. Eventually, half a lifetime of soldiering came to the fore, and Caius slept despite the dull, gray pain of heartache.

꙳ ⚜ ꙳

He was in the forest, searching. Warm brown eyes set in a dusky-skinned face beckoned him forward silently before slipping out of view behind the bole of a massive tree. Caius followed, steadying himself with a child's hand against the rough bark.

It was too quiet... always too quiet in the deep woods. No birds chirped. No leaves rustled. No dapples of ever-shifting sunlight reached the layer of decaying leaves at Caius' feet. He circled the trunk, but the lithe figure with the deep brown eyes was already gone, disappearing behind another tree perhaps ten paces away. Caius crashed through the leaf litter in pursuit, his sandaled footsteps shockingly loud in the muffling silence. Always, his quarry remained just at the edge of vision. A glimpse here, a flicker of movement there – nothing more.

Eventually, a clearing opened ahead of him, and he stumbled to a halt. Clouds choked the sky, turning it flat gray except for a single patch of brilliant blue. A narrow beam of golden sunlight illuminated the trampled grass at the edge of the clearing, where the broken stalks were painted red. A great stag lay crumpled on the ground. Its antlers jutted up like the bare limbs of a dying tree, crimson at the tips. Stripes and splatters of red crisscrossed its tawny coat, three spears jutting obscenely from its body. Its tongue lolled from its open mouth, swollen and dark purple with trapped blood.

Caius didn't want to look at the shapes arrayed around it on the ground. If he looked, it would be real. No, no, no, he chanted, with a child's desperate hope that wishing for something with enough conviction could make it true. He walked forward despite his fervent desire to turn and run away, until the splayed shapes around the fallen stag became men.

Please, no, he thought again, but it didn't make any difference. His feet continued to propel him closer, until *he was standing over the nearest man. A familiar face stared up at the sky sightlessly. Decian's expression had frozen into lines of horror. Sticky blood trailed from a rip in the side of his throat to a puddle drying on the ground. He held no weapon in his hand, but his fingers curled in the air like claws.*

The corpse stared up at him with dead, unblinking eyes, pinning him in place. Caius caught his breath as a blood-red glimmer began to kindle in those brown depths, growing in intensity until the scarlet glow spilled from them like torchlight –

He jolted awake from the dream with a gasp, flailing blindly in the darkness. His elbow thudded against something warm and solid as he scrambled into a sitting position, eliciting a startled grunt from the figure beside him.

"Caius?" A hand closed around his upper arm, half steadying and half restraining. "What is it, what's wrong?"

The dream images dissipated like mist, leaving him clammy with sweat, his heart thudding painfully against his ribs. The rushing noise in his ears resolved itself into the sound of his own gasping breaths.

"*Hey,*" the voice said, and the hand on his arm gave him a little shake. "You were having a nightmare. Come on – wake up."

"I'm all right," Caius croaked, his voice emerging nearly unrecognizable to his own ears.

"Yeah, I can see that," Decian said, not scrimping on the irony. "It must have been quite a dream. Does this happen often?"

Caius swallowed. Once... twice. He licked his lips and shook his head, only to realize that the last of the lamps had gone out at some point, and it was dark as pitch in the room. "No," he managed. "Not... recently, anyway."

If it hadn't been for that thrice-damned hunt — the stag in the forest, staring at him with Kaeto and Bruccias' spears buried in its side...

"It's fine," he said. "I'm fine. I'm sorry I woke you."

The hand that had been gripping his bicep loosened in favor of rubbing up and down his arm before falling away. "Don't worry about it. When I'm sleeping somewhere far away and missing your presence beside me, I'll remind myself of the way you tried to break my ribs with your elbow the first night we spent together."

The choked laugh that broke free of his control sounded wrong, but it was better than any of the other options that might have come out of his mouth.

"Sorry," he said again.

"You should go back to sleep." Decian hesitated. "It's early, but the rain's stopped. I might head back to the kennels now, actually."

Caius' heart still pounded against the inside of his chest, convinced that danger lurked all around. It took him a moment to put Decian's words into context. When he did, his pulse stuttered in response to the sinking feeling in his stomach. He was leaving. It had been their first night... and also their last night. Now it was about to be over.

They would see each other one more time, publicly and with no chance to say or do any of the things they might wish to before their final parting.

"All right," he said faintly.

The silence stretched long enough to grow heavy. His eyes adjusted to the point that he could make out Decian's lean form as a darker shadow amongst the gray of the room.

"All right," Decian echoed eventually.

Warm fingers caught Caius around the nape of the neck and reeled him in. The kiss was clumsy in the dark until Caius' hand blindly found Decian's cheek to steady him. He adjusted the angle, fitting their lips together and taking possession of Decian's mouth. It was a bad idea, since once he'd started he didn't want to stop.

Ever.

After long seconds, they were forced to break for air. Decian ducked his head, resting their foreheads together, his fingers still curled around the back of Caius' neck.

"I'll see you this evening," Decian murmured against his lips.

His hand slid away, and Caius let him go. Decian slid out of the bed, the faint rustling as he found his clothing and pulled it on sounding loud in the dark. He was surefooted in the low light, navigating around the furniture easily. Caius heard him pause at the door.

"Goodbye," Decian said.

Caius found he couldn't answer, and after a moment, Decian left. He lay back in the bed, listening to the sound of the front door being unbarred. It opened and closed, leaving Caius alone in the echoing dark.

TWENTY

Returning to Court would have been a form of torture, even without the knowledge of what was going to happen later in the day. Caius dressed himself with care and dragged his aching body to the main palace, where he was greeted largely with indifference from the various courtiers and adjuncts.

Apparently, the march of days that had passed since the royal hunt had been a sufficient stretch of time for most people to lose interest in the presence of assassins bent on murdering members of the imperial family. Caius wasn't surprised, though he did take more grim satisfaction than was probably seemly in coming up with increasingly ridiculous answers to people asking him where he'd been or what had happened to his leg.

"My horse kicked me. He's always foul-tempered after a hunt," he told the emperor's valet.

"My tailor was adjusting a new pair of trousers to fit, when the needle slipped," he told the wide-eyed head of the armory. "Terrible things, needle sticks—it festered immediately, and the surgeon thought for several days that I might lose the leg."

"An asp bit me. It must have crawled beneath my blankets at night to get warm," he told the adjunct to the treasury. "God knows how it got in the house."

Unfortunately, there were other things to worry about besides scandalizing the palace staff. The date of the Council was almost upon them, with most of the Church dignitaries having already arrived in Amarius. Their presence required significant added security, day and night.

Aelio was at his wits' end, and Caius imagined Laurentin was, as well. The two tribuni were in charge of the palace guard and the city guard, respectively. While their roles didn't often overlap, there was still a degree of rivalry between them at the best of times. Now, they were essentially forced to work together, as the emperor's important guests arrived to find a city in upheaval over their presence.

"If we get through this without a major diplomatic incident, it's going to be a miracle from Deimok himself," Aelio told him privately, as they went over the final plans for security around the formal Council meetings.

They were interrupted by a harried looking pageboy, who bowed low when they turned to him. "Legatus? I come bearing an invitation from the empress. She wishes to speak with you in her private gardens."

Caius and Aelio shared a look. Such a summons was highly unusual, and not something anyone in their right mind would ignore—not unless they harbored a death wish.

"Does she require my presence immediately?" Caius asked.

The page bobbed again. "Yes, Legatus. If you would accompany me?"

Caius turned back to Aelio with a small shrug. "It appears I must take my leave. You might consider redirecting some of the city guard to watch over the larger temples at night. Perhaps we could speak more on the matter tomorrow."

Aelio nodded. "Indeed. I look forward to it."

Caius followed the page through the sprawling interior of the palace, leaving the public areas behind and entering the residential wing. On any other day, he would doubtless be devoting more energy toward wondering about the purpose of the summons. Empress Stasia was not usually a public figure. Caius had met her before, but only in the context of important functions that required her to appear briefly on her husband's arm.

The page led him to a pair of double doors inlaid with colored glass, which opened onto a meticulously appointed garden. The air was perfumed with sweet, floral scents. Flowering plants and elegant statues flanked a path leading to a central area set with stone benches and firepots. There, the empress herself sat primly on one of the seats, looking out across the vista of exotic blooms.

"Your Imperial Majesty," the page said, bowing until his hair nearly brushed the ground. "The legatus is here as you requested."

Stasia turned, taking Caius in with a quick sweep of her pale gray eyes. "Thank you, Jules. You may go."

Her voice was delicate, as was her appearance. She wore an ivory-colored stola—simple in design, but made of rich cloth embroidered with fine designs. Her dark brown hair had been pinned artfully atop her head; soft curls framing her thin face. This was the woman who had wed an emperor... borne him three healthy sons, and managed to avoid falling out of his favor over the course of more than a quarter century.

Idly, Caius wondered what her feelings were regarding the parade of Constanzus' bastards that had entered the palace in recent weeks, never to leave again. Did she even know about them—either of their existence or their fate? Only a fool with very little attachment to his own head would dare to ask such a question.

"Empress," he said, bowing with as much courtly grace as he could manage, given the stiffness of his injury.

"Caius Oppita," she greeted, surprising him with the use of his name rather than his title. "Please... sit."

She indicated another of the benches, and Caius limped over, lowering himself onto it.

"You have saved my husband's life," she said, without further preamble.

"It was my duty," Caius replied by rote, unsure if she were referring the recent hunt, or the battle four years ago. He hesitated before adding, "And it has always been my honor to serve under my emperor's command."

He refused to examine the statement's truthfulness too closely. For years, it *had* been an honor. Constanzus would doubtless go down as one of the great military minds in history. Caius only hoped history would not end up recording a final footnote about the great conqueror's ignominious decline and fall.

"He is not who he once was," Empress Stasia said, eerily echoing his thoughts.

Caius looked up sharply and did not reply, since any reply would either be an admission of disloyalty or a blatant lie.

Stasia waved her hand, dismissing the awkward position in which she'd placed him. "Forgive me, Legatus. You need not answer that, obviously."

"May I ask why you've summoned me here today?" he asked.

She raised an eyebrow. "Is expressing gratitude for your continued service to my husband not reason enough?" The question was coy, and did nothing to settle his misgivings.

"No gratitude is necessary," he told her. "As I said, it is my duty."

Stasia nodded, watching him closely. "Of course. And your duty to the empire is important to you, is it not?"

Oh, what a loaded question that was.

"Yes, Your Imperial Majesty," he said, his voice even.

"What if I were to tell you that the empire now faces a danger greater than it has ever known before?" she asked.

These were turning into deeper waters than Caius was prepared to navigate, on today of all days. He fervently wished he'd slipped away from the palace before the page had managed to find him.

"Then I would express confidence that Alyrios will ultimately prevail, thanks to the strength of its institutions and the loyalty of its citizens." The lie burned against his lips, even as he spoke it.

Stasia tilted her head thoughtfully. "I wish I shared your confidence, Legatus."

Exhaustion washed over him without warning. He was so tired of all this—tired enough that it made him bold. "Please speak plainly, Empress. I fear I am not well-suited to subtle insinuation."

If his recklessness in addressing her in such a way surprised her, she didn't show it. "Tell me your opinion of my sons. One of them will be the next emperor of Alyrios. What do you think of them?"

Fucking hell. Did this endless family scheming extend to the empress as well? He tried not to let the depths of his disquiet show.

"They are ambitious and canny young men," he said neutrally, since saying *'One is a drunkard, one is a terrifying sadist, and one is a slimy arselicker'* probably wouldn't go over too well.

"I have reason to believe that at least one of them is plotting against me," Stasia said, her eyes still burning holes in him.

And... *of course* this meeting would end up being all about her. Not about her husband's reign. Not about the empire. No—one of her sons was plotting against *her*.

"Which one?" he asked.

"I have suspicions, but I do not know for certain." Her brow furrowed. "You are a trusted advisor. I wish to know if any of them have said things to you that you found... unusual or suspect."

Abruptly, he found that he couldn't be done with this conversation fast enough.

"No, Your Imperial Majesty," he lied. "Nothing like that." *Not unless you count their obvious maneuvering to take control of the throne upon their father's death.*

Stasia looked disappointed, as though she'd genuinely expected him to spill some sort of incriminating evidence at her feet. "I see. Very well, Legatus. If you should overhear any useful information related to this matter, I will make it worth your while to pass it on to me. In private, of course."

Yes, of course — I'll get right on that, he thought. Aloud, he only said, "As you wish, Empress. If that is all, I should return to my duties at Court. I've been absent too long as it is."

Stasia looked troubled, but she nodded her assent. "Certainly, Legatus. I don't wish to keep you from the important things you must have to do."

He took his leave from her with another low bow, wondering — not for the first time — what would happen if he purchased passage for two people rather than one at the docks tonight. As always, duty prevented him from giving the idea more than passing consideration.

He'd served Alyrios since he was a lad of seventeen — almost thirty years, now. Somehow, that duty had never felt like such a prison sentence before.

As he'd promised Decian, Caius made his excuses in the middle of the afternoon and left for the day. To maintain appearances, he accepted the offer of a carriage to see him home, even though he could have managed it on foot. As it always had after an injury, getting back to some sense of normalcy acted as better medicine than any tincture or concoction a physician might offer.

Normalcy. He scoffed at himself. There was nothing normal about any of this. He dreaded the coming hours.

As he clambered down from the carriage and approached his front door, a figure on the far side of the street melted into the shadows of an alley between two rows of insulae. Caius took note of the man's presence, but made a point of not staring after him. Clearly, whoever had been following Decian had decided to station a watcher here in anticipation of his return. He wasn't surprised; as he'd said last night, only a fool wouldn't have noticed how much time Decian had been spending here since Caius had been injured.

Let them spy. None of it would matter in a few hours.

Caius had already concocted his cover story, ready for use whenever it might become necessary. Decian was a lively and pleasant drinking companion. He'd lured Caius out for a few hours of merriment in the city despite his sore leg. When Caius was ready to call it a night, Decian expressed the desire to stay out longer, and that was the last Caius had seen or heard from him.

He would suggest moving Pip into the position of houndsman, and bringing in a new lad to work under him. Beyond that, Caius intended to put the whole thing behind him as thoroughly as he could manage. Maybe he'd make good on his threat to spend a night letting Saleene pound the sentimentality out of him, assuming he could afford her rates after giving most of his spare coin to Decian.

He entered the front door, only to find Tertia waiting inside.

"Someone's been watching the house all afternoon," she said by way of greeting. "Should I be worried?"

He sighed. "No. I'll deal with it tonight. It won't be an issue after that, and I guarantee their interest doesn't extend to you, even now."

She held his gaze intently. "You seem very sure of that."

"I am."

Her mouth turned down. "You should take more care, Legatus. Sometimes I worry that you're not as good at these palace games as you think you are."

His face settled into a matching frown. "I don't need to be good at playing them, Tertia. I just need to know how to finish them." He scrubbed a hand through his short hair, tired beyond measure of the whole sorry mess. "Finish up whatever you were doing and go. Everything will be back to normal tomorrow."

He left without waiting for her reply, heading to his room and pointedly closing the door behind him. His sturdy wooden moneybox rested in a concealed compartment in one of the interior walls. The key to the iron padlock securing it was hidden in a specially sewn pouch in one corner of his stupidly soft feather mattress. He hauled out the box and unlocked it, lifting the lid on creaking hinges and assessing its contents.

Money to purchase Decian's passage to safety went into the coin purse hanging at his belt. Most of what was left he poured into a second silk-lined bag, tying it shut and adding that to his belt as well. He locked the box and returned both it and the key to their hiding places. Then he went to test the edges on his sword and his collection of daggers.

Considering the amount of time he'd whiled away sharpening them during the past week, it wasn't surprising that they were all keenly honed. He stowed an extra dagger in his weapons belt and one in each boot. When Decian finally arrived some time later, Caius was in the garden, running through basic sword exercises by torchlight to test the state of his leg—just in case.

"Hullo?" Decian called from outside.

He sheathed his sword and set the sword belt aside for the moment. After limping to the front door to meet him, Caius braced himself against the sight of the younger man's downtrodden expression.

"Hello," Caius said, trying not to remember the lurid details of the previous evening— especially the way Decian had lain relaxed and sated in his bed, curled intimately against his side. "Have you come to drag me out for a drink?"

This, for the benefit of the stableboy who had once again accompanied Decian to help with the horses. Tomorrow, the lad could act as a supporting witness to bolster Caius' story, should such a thing become necessary.

Decian tried on a smile, unconvincing though it was. "You already know me too well," he said. "How's the leg doing?"

"Sore," Caius said, which wasn't a lie. "I had to leave the palace early today to rest it."

"Hmm," Decian mused. "You know what's good for a sore leg? Ale. *Lots of it*. So come with me anyway."

"You certainly do make a persuasive argument," Caius told him, aware of the stable lad watching the exchange with limited interest. "Eh, why not? Give me a minute, and I'll come along despite my better judgment."

He went to retrieve his sword belt from the garden, where he'd left it rather than wearing it to answer the door. After all, he was supposed to be resting — not ready and waiting to leave his house on a moment's notice. With a deep, centering breath, he returned to the entryway — prepared to see this through if it meant Decian would finally be safe from his vengeful half-brother, Kaeto.

"Leg up?" Decian offered, gesturing to Caius' gray gelding.

"Thank you," Caius replied politely. He tried not to notice how his skin tingled where Decian's hands touched him, even through his clothing.

Making it into the saddle was a bit easier today than it had been yesterday. The stableboy held Decian's pony while he, too, clambered up — exhibiting a little more grace than the last time Caius had seen him mount. Caius tossed the stable lad his customary copper coin and sent him on his way. The boy dipped his head in a sloppy bow and jogged off, leaving him alone with Decian... and whoever was watching from the shadows.

"Come on, then," Caius said, wheeling his horse in the direction of the nearest gate leading out of the palace compound. "Let's go see if we can lose ourselves in a tankard."

"And lose anyone following us along the way," Decian muttered, too low to be heard by whoever might be listening.

TWENTY-ONE

The lamplighters had already been out with their long poles, ensuring that the roads running through the sprawling palace compound were lit with flickering orange light. Caius pretended not to be aware of the figure following them on foot. He maintained the easy pace of someone wandering out for a night on the town with a friend, rather than goading his horse into a faster gait in an attempt to outdistance the man behind them.

Decian was a tense presence at his side. Caius could tell that he, too, was making an effort not to look over his shoulder — but he was evidently finding it a struggle. They weren't alone on the streets at this hour, but it wasn't crowded by any means. The mood in the imperial quarter was subdued these days, with the growing unrest and the upcoming Council to worry about.

By rights, Caius should probably be making small talk for the sake of appearances. However, since small talk wasn't a particular skill of his at the best of times, he and Decian rode side by side in grim silence. The only saving grace of the situation was that the awareness of danger helped him push aside the reality of Decian's imminent departure from his life.

The southern gate leading into the city loomed ahead, guarded as always. The portcullis was down, as was generally the case after dark. It would only be lifted for those who had legitimate business inside, and who could prove it—or for those that the guards recognized and trusted. Idly, Caius wondered where the man following them fell along that spectrum.

"Ho, there," called one of the guards, raising a hand as they entered the half-circle of brighter torchlight surrounding the gate. "Who goes there, and what is your business?"

Caius led the way closer and halted his horse. "Legatus Caius Oppita, heading into the city for a few hours with the master of hounds."

"Our business is ale," Decian added, and the guards chuckled.

"Serious business, indeed," said the one on the left. He touched his helm in acknowledgement of Caius' rank. "A good evening to you, Legatus. Houndsman."

Without fuss, he gestured to the men stationed at the gate mechanism. They turned the massive crank, machinery creaking as the heavy portcullis rose. Decian watched it nervously despite his earlier witty quip, as though worried that someone would drop it on their heads as they tried to pass through.

Caius nodded to the guards. "Thank you, guardsmen. We'll be back at some point, I expect." *Or one of us will be, at any rate.*

"I'll let the next shift know," said the man, giving another small salute as he and Decian rode past.

Behind them, Caius heard the gate clank as it was closed. It was possible that would be that, as far as their pursuer went... but Caius had been a soldier for a very long time before becoming a palace lapdog, and he wasn't about to assume things would be so easy.

"Come on," he said, urging his gelding into a jog. "We wouldn't want the Wooly Ram to run out of ale before we get there."

He glanced around to see Decian gritting his teeth as he jounced up and down in time with the pony's jarring trot. Caius' bad leg was none too pleased about the faster pace, either, but the sooner they left the open area surrounding the walls of the imperial quarter and lost themselves in the dim streets and alleys of Amarius, the happier he'd be.

The open space was specifically designed to leave anyone approaching the imperial quarter without cover. It had never been put to a military test in the city's long and storied history, but Caius could now confirm that it succeeded in its stated purpose of making him feel uncomfortably exposed.

On the positive side, the lack of cover made it easy enough to be sure that they were not, in fact, being followed by anyone from within the palace compound. Their shadow from earlier hadn't exited through the gate after them.

"We'll head in the general direction of the Wooly Ram," Caius said, confident no one was within hearing range. "Once we get into a busier area, we can make for the backstreets and take an indirect route to the docks."

Decian gave a tight nod.

The first buildings appeared on either side of the vaia along which they were riding. This area was an administrative district—a quiet place after dark, with all the bureaucrats either resting at home or frequenting the bars and taverns in the southern quarter. The cobbled road was wide and well kept, lit sparingly with street lamps that left large swathes of shadow between the pools of flickering illumination.

From the distance, the sounds of a restless city reached their ears as an undifferentiated din. Caius' horse tossed his head and shied a step sideways as they passed the first of the towering marble edifices. The fine hair on the back of his neck prickled. He cast a glance at the dark space between one building and the next, but could make out nothing.

He looked up to assess the sky. Lingering clouds leftover from the previous night's rain obscured the moon, which would otherwise be waxing gibbous tonight. On a clear evening, it might have offered enough light to be useful, though the buildings would still cast dark shadows. As it was, the darkness beyond the reach of the street lamps was impenetrable.

"Look sharp," he murmured, maintaining a brisk pace toward the more frequented areas of the city that lay ahead. As the buildings became shabbier and the streets around them more active, Caius cast his senses outward with the wariness of the battlefield.

"There are hoofbeats coming from behind us," Decian said, still maintaining the kind of stiff posture that said he was working very hard not to crane around and look over his shoulder.

"I'm well aware," Caius replied grimly. "Don't worry... we're getting into an area where it will be easier to disappear into the alleyways and circle around."

The port was on the northern edge of the city. Caius had purposely left by the south gate, heading toward the southern quarter to further confuse anyone who might be following. That did, however, mean that they would have to travel the entire breadth of the city to get where they were going. Fortunately, the docks never slept. Sailors and longshoremen would still be about their business after even the most tenacious drunkards had abandoned the taverns for the night.

From the sound of it, there were at least two riders on their tail, which was worrying. Something about the entire situation niggled at his instincts. If Kaeto or anyone else suspected Decian of being an escaped prisoner, why not simply arrest him at the kennels and drag him before a tribunal?

Aspects of the situation made no sense, and Caius *hated* things that made no sense.

Now, though, they were entering a narrower street lined with shops and inns. The Wooly Ram was located off an intersection perhaps three blocks away, and they were no longer the only people of horseback. Some distance ahead, Caius could make out the familiar sounds of chanting.

"Sounds like our pagan friends are back," Decian said. "Can you tell if those riders are still behind us?"

Caius frowned. "They'd have to be complete incompetents to have lost us already."

If the protest ahead was large enough, it would add to the confusion and might aid them in slipping away. If it was *too* large, there was a risk of getting bogged down—hemmed in by an angry crowd. He headed for the noise anyway, trusting to their ability to skirt around it on horseback rather than getting caught up.

"If there's a crowd around the protest, we'll mix with the edges and use the confusion as cover to disappear into an alley," he said. "If we can make it a couple of roads over without being seen, we should be able to slip away and head north for the docks."

Decian nodded his understanding, clenching his pony's reins with determination.

Two blocks ahead, they did indeed run into the back of a crowd of gawkers gathering to watch the protest. Most were on foot, which was less than ideal for use as cover, but there were a few carts and wagons mixed in, along with a handful of other riders. Were he not still recovering from his leg wound, he would have been sorely tempted to ditch the horses at that point... but he was, and they would have a lot of ground to cover to reach the docks.

He contented himself with trying to use the shadows to their advantage as they wove between wagons and drays, getting as far into the confusion of excited people as they dared without attracting too much attention. Before long, Caius slipped into an alley running between two large buildings, with Decian right on his heels.

The alley led to a smaller road one block over. Caius turned onto it only long enough to find another alley leading to an even more disreputable looking street. "Now we're getting somewhere," he muttered.

Decian looked around. "This is definitely… somewhere."

The houses surrounding them were dingy and ill kept, some of them leaning drunkenly at odd angles. Caius led the way to an intersection and turned left, their horses' hooves plop-plopping through puddles of filth in the road. At the next intersection he turned right, aware that they were entering an older area of the city where the roads did not meet at neat right angles, but wound around curves and bends with little logic.

They rounded one such bend, only to be confronted by two riders standing at the next crossroads, facing them with swords in hand. Caius felt a moment of disbelief, quickly lost in an instinctive rush of battle-readiness leftover from years of campaigning. Their pursuers should not have been able to get in front of them. Not unless they had the demons' own luck. It seemed… physically impossible.

"Back the way we came," he snapped, aware that this was a far worse area for a confrontation than someplace with crowds and witnesses.

He wheeled his horse; Decian yanked the pony around beside him. Two more riders appeared in the intersection they'd just passed through, and Caius felt his stomach drop.

"Alley," he ordered, riding for the nearest gap between rows of slatternly houses.

Decian cursed under his breath and followed. The previous night's rain had turned the garbage-strewn ground in the alley to muck, the horses feet slipping in it as they turned into the claustrophobic space.

The clouds chose that moment to part, moonlight spilling in from above. It illuminated two more riders as they entered the far end of the alley, blocking it. Caius' heart sank, even as he reached right-handed for his sword hilt and drew steel. He looked over his shoulder just as the four riders from the road entered behind them, pinning them.

Caius met Decian's wide eyes. "We're charging the two at the other end," he said in the calmest tone he could muster, painfully aware of how poor their odds were against even two armed opponents... much less six. "Stay behind me as best you can. If you see a chance to get past them, take it. Don't let them unhorse you unless it's unavoidable."

"This is a horrible plan!" Decian said, wrestling with the nervous pony's reins. "*Why are all of your plans horrible?*"

Unfortunately, Caius didn't have an answer to that. Time was not their friend, so he pointed his gelding at the far end of the alley and dug his heels in. The horse half-reared, startled, and bolted forward. The gray wasn't battle-trained—Caius could only hope the same was true of their enemies' mounts. Already, the gelding was hesitating, wary of rushing directly at a pair of unfamiliar animals in the dark.

Caius slapped it sharply on the haunches with the flat of his sword, sending it scrambling forward again in the slippery muck. He dared a quick glance behind him in the moonlight. Decian was kicking the pony in the ribs, urging the reluctant beast after Caius' mount. The other four riders had already entered the alley, two abreast, preparing to pincer them.

All Caius could do was commit to the strategy he'd initiated. With a roar, he lifted his sword and propelled his mount into the other two. In the brief moment before the clash, familiar battle-lust sang in his veins, banishing the aches of age and injury.

Horseflesh thudded against horseflesh. The rider on the right took most of the brunt of the impact as the other horse skittered sideways. Caius' sword was already in motion, but the terrible footing betrayed him. Both animals' legs went out from under them, sending horses and riders alike to the ground in a tangle.

Caius kicked free and rolled, aware of the shriek of agony from his injured leg. The pain was distant. Unimportant, because to acknowledge his body's condition would result in the battle being lost before it had properly started. These men weren't playing. It was pretty clear that if Caius didn't prevail in this fight, he wouldn't be in a position to feel pain — or anything else — ever again.

He stumbled to his feet, covered in filth but with his sword hilt still gripped firmly in his right hand. The gray gelding staggered upright and bolted from the alley, disappearing from sight. The other horse was still down, legs flailing without coordination, its rider trapped beneath it.

One down.

Caius parried a clumsy strike from the second rider. "Go! *Go!*" he shouted at Decian, forcing his opponent into a defensive block with a wild slash.

To his immense relief, Decian kicked and prodded his terrified mount through the gap Caius had made, barely avoiding the downed horse's thrashing legs. There might be more men waiting beyond the alley mouth, but that was not something he could control. For now, Decian was free. Caius just had to keep the five remaining combatants from getting past him to pursue the aging pony with their faster mounts.

He ducked to avoid a slash that would have taken his head off, cursing both the horrible footing and his leg's weakness. Grabbing the dagger from his belt with his bad arm, he distracted his opponent with a right-handed sword lunge. The man parried, and Caius took the opening to drive the dagger point into his calf muscle. The move pushed the boundaries of his strength and range of motion on that side, but it was enough to make the rider cry out and curl instinctively toward the injury — at which point Caius' sword edge took him across the throat.

Unfortunately, the other four attackers were already upon him, even before the dead man's body slid from the saddle. There was only room for two of them to engage him at once in the narrow space, but even so, his options were limited. He grabbed the reins of the horse whose rider he'd just dispatched, dragging the animal in front of him to use as a physical barrier. His bad shoulder screamed in protest at the strain as he yanked the beast into position, but the front two riders pulled up, unable to get within sword-range.

The panicked horse he was holding bucked and plunged in the confined space, trying to get free. Caius held onto it grimly. Metal flashed in moonlight and it staggered, blood spraying from its throat. With a gurgling scream, the animal stumbled to its knees and collapsed, its body floundering as it rapidly bled out.

The two riders in front dismounted and climbed over the twitching horse on foot, weapons raised. Caius backed away, his own sword held ready even as he reached for one of his boot daggers with his left hand. He was limited in how much ground he could afford to surrender before he hit the end of the alley. Honestly, his chances of survival might be better in the open, but as soon as the battle spilled into the street, there was nothing to stop the two remaining riders from going after Decian.

"Who are you? Who sent you?" he growled. He didn't hold out much hope of getting them talking as a distraction. He didn't hold out much hope, *period*. Still, every second's delay was one more second's head start for Decian.

Unsurprisingly, the men did not reply.

"Stop dallying, you pair of cretins," said one of the riders. "*Take him.*"

The two on foot attacked in unison. Caius blocked and dodged, dreading the moment when his leg would fail him or his feet would slip in the muck at the wrong instant. *Parry, lunge, whirl, retreat... keep them both in front... don't let them get past and out of the alley.*

It started to go wrong almost immediately. His heel hit one of the downed horses' legs as he gave ground—not hard enough to make him stumble, but enough to rob his parry of power as his center of balance shifted unexpectedly. The rhythm of the two-on-one fight faltered. He jerked one opponent's sword to the side, but the movement left an opening for the other that was outside the range of motion of the parrying dagger held with his bad arm.

He braced for the strike, teeth gritted, only for the man to go down with a cry under the force of a dark, heavy shape. Whatever it was, it had barreled past Caius without slowing, running low to the ground. The remaining horses in the alley screamed in terror, rearing and bolting toward the opposite end. One of the riders fell to the ground with a grunt, unseated. The other rider struggled to regain control and galloped away, fleeing the scene.

Eerie red eyes and sharp teeth gleamed in the moonlight as the attacking creature savaged Caius' downed opponent. The sight almost made him drop his guard against the second swordsman. Fortunately, the other man was just as shocked as he was — unable to take advantage of the opening.

Caius pushed past his clamoring instincts as they shouted *bad, wrong, get away*, and managed a clumsy swing that caught his opponent in the side. Blood spurted, and Caius jammed his dagger through the man's ribcage before kicking him to the ground. He whirled toward the thing with the red eyes, his weapons raised defensively.

The… *creature*… seemed almost to glow in the darkness — a wavering aura like phosphorus light surrounding its pitch-black hide. Its eyes were burning coals, lit from within. It was doglike in outline, but larger and more heavily muscled than any dog Caius had ever seen in his life.

It held its victim's throat clamped in its jaws, shaking the downed man like a terrier with a rat. As Caius watched in horror, the beast's outline seemed to shift and separate into two. A ghostly, translucent version plunged muzzle-deep into its victim's chest. Its jaws snapped closed, and it dragged out a shimmering smear of a shape. There was no substance to the wavering, smoke-like figure, but dark holes forming the shape of eyes and a mouth opened in a silent, existential scream. The spirit-hound snarled and flung the diaphanous form into the void. As it disappeared, the man's physical body abruptly went limp within the creature's grip.

TWENTY-TWO

The thing lifted its bloody jaws, the ghostly form and the physical form merging into one. Its glowing eyes pinned the unlucky man who'd fallen when his mount bolted moments before. Caius stumbled backward to put distance between them, tripping over the tangled limbs of one of the dead horses. Agony flared in his leg as his arse landed in the muck. He clutched his weapons in a tight grip, unable to properly feel his fingers. His mouth hung open in shock, every single thought frozen in solid ice as he watched the hellhound lunge for the injured rider.

The man made a clumsy swing for the creature with his sword, only to scream as massive jaws closed around his forearm and bore him down. The screams grew louder, and again the strange double-vision image of the physical hound and the ghostly hound separated. As before, the ghost hound ripped something intangible and essential from its victim's body, flinging it into the darkness.

The man slumped, obviously dead. Silence fell over the alley, broken only by Caius' harsh gasps and the pained groaning of the attacker still trapped under his horse.

The hellhound looked up from its dispatched prey, its red eyes falling on Caius. Every hair on his body stood up, gooseflesh shivering across his skin as that unearthly gaze met his. A sense of something weighty and unavoidable thickened the night air. Caius' numb fingers tightened on the sword.

The two stared at each other, moonlight limning the scene with silver. As Caius watched, the beast's outline twisted, reality shifting around it until a human figure crouched opposite him in the alley's filth. Red light spilled from the man's eyes, and Caius' heart stuttered, skipping a beat before pounding painfully into triple time. In that instant, he was transported back to the forest of his youth — staring at a dead shapeshifter as his father's corpse cooled in the grass nearby. Caius forced himself to his feet, ignoring the treacherous weakness in his knees as terror and hot rage flooded him in equal measure.

The crimson glow faded from the shapeshifter's eyes, and Decian looked up at him. He was naked, surrounded by bodies, with human blood running down his chin. Nausea slammed into Caius' gut as images of kissing those gore-stained lips played across his mind's eye. When his awareness flickered back to the present, he was standing with his sword under Decian's chin, and he couldn't quite remember putting it there.

"You," Caius rasped. "You're... you're a..."

He couldn't get the words out.

Decian lifted his chin, the bite of the blade having forced him up to his knees. "Caius," he began.

"*Shapeshifter*," Caius hissed, the sound like a curse.

The moon was too bright. He didn't want to see the details of this; didn't want to see the way Decian's brown eyes shone with a look of betrayal as he knelt, disheveled and bloody, with Caius' weapon at his throat.

"Caius," Decian said again. "Please... I don't understand what's happening to me. Before, with the dogs—"

In a flash as bright and abrupt as a lightning strike, Caius remembered Decian crouched naked among the royal hounds, safe and untouched as they savaged their caretaker. He remembered the unnatural way the beasts had submitted to him, practically abasing themselves to avoid antagonizing him.

"*What are you?*" he demanded, distantly aware that his grip on the sword hilt was trembling.

"I don't know!" Decian said. "That's what I'm trying to tell you! That day in the kennels... that was the first time it's ever happened. And this was the second! Caius—*I don't know what this is!*"

"You're an abomination," Caius whispered hoarsely. "A killer."

The look of betrayal grew deeper for a moment, before Decian's expression settled into blank lines. His lip curled into a bitter half-smile, made grotesque by the blood on his face.

"An abomination." The words were a low monotone. "And after all of this, will I die now at your hands, soldier?" he asked, echoing the question he'd posed when Caius had found him alive among the dogs, having miraculously survived his own execution.

After his father's death... after the slaughter on an Eburosi beach... Caius had vowed that if any shapeshifter ever ended up beneath the point of his sword, he would run the bastard through without a second thought. He stared down at his lover. His secret. His *act of treasonous justice.*

... and he could not move the blade a finger's width. His stomach cramped, churning with a poisonous slurry of grief, self-loathing, and bitter anger.

"Go," he said. The word tasted like bile. "Leave Amarius. Leave the empire, and don't look back. Because if I ever see you again, I'll kill you."

"*Caius.*" Decian's voice was pleading.

"*Don't.*" Caius jerked the sword up a fraction, forcing Decian's head back. "Don't use my name. Don't look at me like I should somehow have mercy on *what you are.*" His voice rose to a shout. "Go! *Get out of my sight, damn you!*"

Decian scrambled upright, away from the sword at his throat, and fled the alley.

Caius stood frozen, breath coming in great, shuddering gasps. He wanted to collapse in a heap on the filthy ground, but he was afraid if he did, he might not get up again. Almost against his will, practicalities began to flutter and peck at the edge of his awareness. One of the attackers had fled the scene. It was conceivable he might eventually return with reinforcements.

He turned slowly, following the sound of weak groaning. The trapped rider was still alive, his leg pinned beneath the crushing weight of his dead horse. The animal's neck was broken, snapped during the fall. Caius channeled all of his bitter rage and betrayal into his trembling muscles, forcing them into action. He limped toward the man, sheathing his sword along the way. After kicking the fallen rider's sword out of reach, he fell to his knees, grabbed the brigand by the hair, and jerked his head around.

"Who sent you?" he demanded, barely recognizing his own voice.

The man clenched his jaw, panting shallowly past the pain of his crushed leg.

Caius let his head go in favor of pinning his left wrist with a knee. Ignoring the muck coating the ground, he grabbed the man's thumb and sawed through it with his dagger, feeling the joint crack as the tendons gave way. Screams echoed against the walls of the tenement buildings.

"Who sent you?" he asked again.

The man flopped like a fish. Caius grabbed his index finger and twisted it until it broke.

"Who sent you?"

"I don't know!" the man shrieked, snot and spittle flying in the moonlight.

Caius twisted his middle finger until it snapped, then waited until the fresh round of high-pitched screaming subsided into whimpers.

"Try harder," he suggested.

"I d-don't know, I swear!" The man choked and gagged for a moment before regaining control of his voice. "The orders c-came anonymously. That's how they always come!"

Caius changed tack. "Did your paymaster know Decian was a shapeshifter? Is that why they came after him?"

The man stared up at him, sniveling and bewildered. "Who?"

"The houndsman!" Caius snapped, and broke the man's ring finger, setting off another round of hoarse screams. "Did they know he was a shapeshifter when they sent you after him, *yes or no*?"

The man's eyes were growing hazy with pain, but the confusion in his face was unsettlingly real. "We weren't after him!" he gasped. "We were after you!"

Caius blinked, going utterly still as the events of the last couple of weeks reshuffled themselves in his mind, like a child's painted puzzle pieces coming together to form a completely new picture.

The assassins in the woods.

The shadowy figure outside the Cock's Crow.

The men stationed outside his house to monitor any comings and goings.

Oh.

Oh.

Dear god. *He was such a fool.*

Wrenching free of his sudden paralysis, he looked down at the shuddering man trapped beneath him. "Right," he said. "That makes sense. Well, I can only hope you got paid up front."

Grabbing the man's hair again, Caius forced his head back and slit his throat with a single, efficient slice. He let the body fall, convulsing in the mud, and forced himself to unsteady feet. Every single square inch of his body ached—a welcome distraction from the sharp pain in his heart that throbbed and pulsed fresh blood with every beat.

Calling on three decades of battle experience, he packed that pain into a tight, dark ball and put bars around it, resolving not to spare another thought for the dangerous shapeshifting warlock he'd unknowingly let into his bed. Into his *life*. Decian would either run, and Caius would never hear from him again… or he'd succumb to his dark nature and kill more people, in which case the Amarian guard would hunt him down.

Either way, he wasn't Caius' problem any longer. Now, he had a *new* problem. Someone inside the palace apparently wanted him dead, and was prepared to go to extraordinary lengths to make that happen. Battle fatigue dragged at him as he trudged to the end of the alley, heavily favoring his left leg.

He looked around warily, but there was no sign of Decian. In a much-needed burst of good fortune, he found his gelding wandering aimlessly in the roadway perhaps two hundred paces away. To his relief, the horse did not attempt to flee when Caius approached and caught him. The animal was caked in mud, bleeding sluggishly from scrapes and cuts along his right side, but he appeared sound otherwise.

The shutters of all the houses along the street were tightly and pointedly closed. In this area, the clash of a sword battle and the screams of someone being tortured were clearly a reason to huddle inside with the doors locked, rather than venturing out to investigate. All of which meant that Caius was on his own when it came to mounting his damned horse so he could ride away.

He looked at the saddle, which might as well have retreated to a distant mountaintop when it came to how accessible it appeared from the ground. There was nothing nearby to use as a mounting block. For lack of any other options, Caius dragged himself onto the animal's back mostly by virtue of willpower, his vision wavering in and out for a disconcerting few moments as his leg protested the exertion.

He was aware that more assassins could appear at any time. If they did, he was as good as dead. With this thought firmly in mind, he rode toward the distant sound of shops and taverns and *people*, making for the most crowded area he could find. Once he had his bearings and was safely surrounded by witnesses who might object to someone being assaulted in the street for no reason, he doggedly headed for the imperial quarter, riding for the same gate he and Decian had left by.

There was a degree of fierce stubbornness involved in his decision to return to his own quarters rather than attempting to flee—but it was not the irrational decision it might have appeared on the surface. Had the emperor himself wanted Caius dead, he would have ordered him arrested at his home, or inside the palace when he was attending the Imperial Court. Whoever was after him, Caius was confident they didn't have official sanction. Moreover, they obviously wanted the deed to occur somewhere far away from the palace, where it might be easier to convince people that his death was an unfortunate random act.

The guards at the gate were the same ones from earlier in the evening, and they reacted with alarm at the sight of him and his horse, muddy and blood-covered.

"Send a boy to my house to take my horse back to the stables and care for him," he ordered.

"Sir," said the guard who'd spoken to them when they'd left. "You weren't alone earlier. What of the houndsman?"

"I wasn't alone then, it's true," he agreed in a flat tone. "But I am now."

The man didn't push for an explanation, either out of respect for Caius' rank, or because he looked like he was in danger of falling out of the saddle at any moment. Caius passed beneath the portcullis and headed for his residence, only vaguely curious as to whether someone would be lurking outside to take note of his arrival.

His *survival*.

Indeed, as he approached his front door, movement in the shadows across the street registered in his peripheral vision. He ignored it, trusting to his earlier assessment that if his unknown nemesis thought they could get away with having him killed here, they'd have done so long ago. Dismounting was not quite as fraught as mounting had been, but he had to clutch the saddle for a moment until his knees agreed to take his weight. Once he was steady, he tied the horse outside for the stableboy to collect and let himself in the front door.

His house was eerily unchanged from a couple of hours ago when he'd left. It felt as though everything should be upended, torn apart and thrown to the four winds. He shrugged off the irrational feeling and limped toward his bedroom, unbuckling his weapons belt as he went. It was heavy with the coins he hadn't thought to give Decian before he'd driven the younger man away. With the door closed behind him, Caius shed what muddy, filth-encrusted clothing he could. He managed to get his boots off with the help of the boot-pull, but the trousers defeated him.

The bottles of wine in the kitchen called to him, but he resisted their siren lure. Enough wine might help with the clamoring pain of muscles and joints pushed past their endurance, but he'd need his head clear in a few hours. Instead, he slumped onto the ridiculous feather mattress, letting his aching body sink into it. Drawing from the same deep well of stubbornness that had allowed him to haul himself onto his horse's back after the battle, he closed his eyes and banished the events of the evening to a dark corner of his mind.

Thankfully, he still possessed the soldier's skill of sleeping whenever the opportunity arose, no matter what else might be occurring at the time. Unfortunately, that talent did nothing to prevent the nightmares from coming, even if his body's exhaustion ensured that he did not wake from them. He lay in bed, alone, twitching as dream images tortured him behind his eyelids. Outside, the moon that had illuminated horrors both earthly and unearthly in an unremarkable Amarian alley slid slowly across the western sky.

When morning came, there would be a reckoning… whether Caius was ready for it or not.

TWENTY-THREE

Decian fled the blood-soaked alley, scrubbing madly at his face and jaw with muddy hands. Inside his chest, something horrible swelled. If it broke free, he wasn't sure what would happen — whether he would wail, or weep, or stand in the middle of the street and scream at the sky until his throat bled.

He was naked. The beast had taken over his mind and body again, pressing his humanity aside — filling the space with something... *other*. And then Caius —

Decian's breathing stuttered, growing fast and shallow.

No. He quashed the memory, instead casting his gaze around the street until he found the pile of torn fabric that had, up until recently, been his clothing. The shirt had been reduced to rags. The trousers were ripped — almost shredded in places — but he pulled them on anyway. His boots were intact. He tugged them onto his bare, muddy feet, since he couldn't find his stockings.

The sobering realization that he had no idea where he was — and no idea where he could go — washed over him like cold water. In the next instant, a scream of agony echoed from the alley mouth. Decian whirled toward the sound, heart pounding. Seconds later it came again, desperate and high-pitched.

He cursed himself for thinking that it might be Caius screaming. Caius had been fine a few moments ago — on his feet, angry and armed. One of the men who'd attacked them had still been pinned under his horse, injured and unable to get free.

More shrieks echoed, interspersed with the sound of choking and retching.

Caius had called *Decian* a killer, and now he was dragging those sounds from the throat of an injured man. Decian's stomach turned over. With no other options that didn't involve the threat of immediate death beneath his lover's sword, he turned his back on the shrieks and started walking. Ahead, Caius' gray gelding paced restlessly near the next intersection. Decian slowed. He briefly considered stealing the horse before deciding that even if he could successfully catch the animal and scramble onto its tall back, he probably wouldn't be able to control it.

He reluctantly passed the gelding by and turned right at the intersection, heading toward the distant sounds of human activity. He'd barely gone twenty paces when his eyes lit on a fat pair of haunches and a scruffy tail poking out from between two buildings. The pony radiated tense sullenness, resembling nothing so much as one of the giant flightless birds from Kulawi that his mother used to tell him stories about, which dealt with danger by sticking their heads in the sand so they couldn't see the threat coming.

"Hey, you," Decian said hoarsely, approaching the pony's pudgy rear end with caution. True to form, it didn't move or acknowledge him in any way, so he squeezed past it to reach its head. The pony's reins had snapped at some point, possibly because it had stepped on them in its haste to get away. The two ends were still attached to the bit, however, so he tied them together and urged the animal backwards, out of its ridiculous hiding place.

The pony complied with mulishly pinned ears. Its lips curled in disdain as Decian checked the girth and gathered up the reins, but it didn't try to evade him as he stuck a foot in the stirrup and levered himself onto its back. He directed it toward the sounds of life coming from the distant business district, keeping a nervous eye out for additional attackers lurking in the shadows.

There was, he decided in short order, really only one place he could go. He had no money, no food, no water, and his clothing—what there was of it—was in tatters. Saleene's brothel would only be a haven for him as long as Caius didn't show up to tell them what had happened... and that assumed they'd even let him through the door in the first place. But it was still something, and without it, he had nothing.

If his nebulous idea to seek shelter and assistance there didn't work out, he would have to try to sell the pony—and hope no one realized it had been stolen from the imperial stables. He wasn't even sure what kind of money the little beast would bring—being locked in prison for a decade wasn't exactly conducive to staying on top of the latest livestock prices.

He rode through the city for some time, looking for any familiar landmarks that he could use to orient himself. Finally, he stumbled across the road leading to the Wooly Ram, and from there he was able to find the Vaia Condora and the gymnaestra he'd visited with Caius. After that, it wasn't too difficult to retrace the route they'd taken to the Cock's Crow. Good gods, had it only been *yesterday*? Surely that was impossible...

He tied the pony outside the building, trying to ignore the strange looks he was getting from passersby. Bare-chested and with gaping holes ripped in his trousers, he'd be lucky if he wasn't arrested by the nearest city guard for being a vagrant, or a public nuisance or something. Rather than attempting to enter through the front, he skirted around the side of the building, trying to ignore the frisson of disquiet he felt at once again being in a darkened alley.

The side door was unlocked, so he ducked inside the tavern and made for the unobtrusive interior door at the back. Caius had said that Saleene and Zuri's brothel was located above the Cock's Crow, and since there had been no staircase visible in the front of the house, it stood to reason this must be the way in.

Or... it might be the kitchen. That was also a possibility.

He poked his head in, ready to duck out of the way to avoid being mowed down by a serving wench carrying a loaded tray. Inside lay a quiet parlor rather than a busy kitchen, populated by a bored looking young man who looked vaguely familiar, along with a pair of pretty girls wearing sheer, thigh-length stolas and nothing else.

The oddly familiar young man looked up and frowned. "Come in if you're coming."

Decian stepped through the door sheepishly, and the man's frown deepened. The girls tittered nervously at his half-clothed, mud-spattered appearance. He took a moment to be thankful that any blood on him would have dried to a rusty, unremarkable brown by now—or else the girls would doubtless have been doing more than giggling at him.

Even so, the man rose, stepping forward aggressively, and it was only then that Decian finally placed him. He was the one from the gymnaestra, that Caius had called Saleene's *pretty boy*.

"Nuh-uh," he was saying. "No way. You can't come in here looking like that. You've got no money, you get no girls. *Out*."

"Wait," Decian said breathlessly. "I'm not here for that. I need to speak to either Zuri or Saleene— it's important!"

"Yeah, *sure* it is," said the pretty boy, slapping a hand flat against Decian's chest and shoving him back a step. "I said, *out*."

Decian gritted his teeth, scrambling for any kind of a story that might get him past the gatekeeper.

"Stop!" he insisted. "Look—you saw me at the gymnaestra yesterday with the legatus, right?

Caius? He's the one who sent me here! He's in trouble, and I urgently need to get a message to your employers on his behalf!"

The pretty boy hesitated, wavering.

"*Please*," Decian pressed. "I'm begging you—it's life or death!"

The girls had been watching the exchange curiously. After that dramatic declaration, one of them spoke up.

"I could take him to one of the empty rooms and let Saleene know he's here once she's done with her client," she said. "Caius has been coming here for years, and this sounds serious, Tullio."

Pretty boy—*Tullio*—chewed his lip for a moment before giving her a reluctant nod. "Yeah, I guess."

Decian let out the breath he'd been holding. "Thank you," he whispered.

The woman rose gracefully from her seat and gave him a wary look as she slipped past him, heading for the staircase at the back of the room.

"Not so fast," Tullio said as he made to follow her. "You got any weapons on you?"

Decian gestured at himself. "Are you joking? I don't even have a damned *shirt*."

Tullio only grunted skeptically, and Decian submitted without comment to having his boots and waistband checked for hidden blades.

"Come on," said the girl, once Tullio waved him on.

He followed her upstairs to an empty room furnished with a bed, a chair, and a divan. She left him there and closed the door behind her. Decian heard a lock click. He lowered himself gingerly onto the chair, painfully aware of how filthy he was, and settled in to wait — one leg jiggling impatiently.

Time dragged. He wasn't sure how long it had been when the lock finally turned and the door opened, admitting Zuri. She took one look at him and scowled.

"Great ancestor spirits, whatever has befallen you?" she asked, closing the door again to give them privacy.

Decian opened his mouth, only to realize that he had no earthly idea what should come out of it. A choked noise emerged instead of words, and he wrapped his arms around himself as he realized that tears had started running down his cheeks. Mortified, he turned his face away from her, trying to get hold of his emotions. Fingers grasped his jaw, forcing him to lift his gaze and meet her dark brown eyes.

"I'm sorry," he whispered. "I didn't know where else to go. It's all gone wrong…"

"I can see that," Zuri said wryly, taking in his battered appearance. "Are you injured?"

He shook his head back and forth within the confines of her grip, and she let him go. The magnitude of everything he'd just lost hit him anew. His eyes burned almost painfully as the intensity of his grief threatened to escape its cage, and Zuri breathed in sharply, straightening away from him in surprise.

She opened her mouth to speak, but the sound of someone else entering the room interrupted her.

Saleene swept in, her expression hard-edged. She was fully dressed, but the smell of sex clung to her as she strode up to Decian and loomed over him.

"What's happened?" she demanded. "I just got a garbled message about Caius, and a matter of life and death. Start talking. Where is he?"

"I don't know," Decian said wretchedly. "I'm sorry. Six men attacked us in an alley, but as far as I know he's all right. They... they were after me, not him."

Saleene's expression turned even grimmer. "Ah. So the chickens have come home to roost, then. If he survived, why didn't he come here with you?"

A tight band settled around Decian's chest, constricting his breathing. "We... fought, afterward," he managed, aware of how inadequate the word was when it came to describing what had happened. "He sent me away, and I didn't know where else to go. I can't go back to the palace—I'd be killed on sight."

Saleene's gray eyes narrowed. "You fought off six men and then had a *lovers' quarrel*?"

Decian swallowed, painfully aware that there was nothing he could tell her that wouldn't dig himself deeper into a hole. "... yes?"

She crossed her arms, staring down at him from her considerable advantage of height. "You're lying about something—or omitting something, at the very least. And I have limited patience for liars."

Zuri had been watching the exchange closely, but now she spoke up. "Haartlam," she said, addressing Saleene, "we need to take him in."

Saleene looked at her sharply. "What? Zuri, I'm not in the business of cosseting jilted lovers. If you want to give him a few coins to buy some clothes and a meal, that's one thing—"

"No," Zuri said evenly. "You're not listening, my love. We *need* to take him in."

Saleene stared at her, and Zuri held her gaze with a meaningful look. An entire wordless conversation seemed to pass between the pair—one that Decian wasn't privy to. Eventually, Saleene blinked.

"You can have a room and two meals a day in exchange for cleaning and odd jobs," she told Decian, though her eyes never left Zuri. "*For now.*"

Decian's chest hitched on a shudder of relief. Even so, he couldn't help picking at the scab. "And if Caius comes here?" he asked.

"I have no earthly idea," Saleene said with brutal honesty. "One thing at a time. Go clean yourself up. I wasn't born yesterday, and not all of that mess on you is mud. Zuri can show you the bathing area and find you some clothes. After which, she and I need to have a talk."

For her part, Zuri seemed unfazed by Saleene's rather dire tone. "That we do, beloved. Come on, Decian. Let's get you cleaned up and find you a place to sleep. You look like you need it."

He nodded, exhaustion washing over him as though her words had conjured it from thin air. "Thank you. Thank you both. I came here on a pony — it's tied up outside. Is there anyplace it can be cared for and fed for the night?"

"I'll have Tullio see to it," Zuri said. "Don't worry. Now... follow me."

Decian rose beneath Saleene's watchful eye and did as he was told, feeling some tiny fraction of the tension in his shoulders begin to unravel. It was a precarious perch — but at least he'd found someplace safe to land, rather than crashing headfirst into his own grave.

TWENTY-FOUR

Outside Caius' bedroom window, dawn painted the street golden. He lay on his back, covered in bruises and scrapes, every joint and muscle feeling like a wagon wheel that had been neglected too long and rusted into immobility.

Decian was a murderous, shapeshifting hellhound who could rip men's souls from their bodies and fling them into the void.

Someone inside the palace wanted Caius dead.

His thoughts circled back and forth between the two catastrophic revelations, making no headway toward dealing with either one. What had he ever done to deserve either of these things? He'd never asked for a lover. Never wanted one, since Serah had died and left him alone. It was outrageous to think that he'd somehow fallen for the same kind of unnatural creature that had butchered his father when he was a mere boy.

And the imperial family. He'd served them faithfully for well over half his life. He'd sacrificed his blood to keep them safe, and he carried the scars to prove it. Until mere weeks ago when he'd spared Decian's life, he had never once questioned them; never defied them or worked against their aims.

It had to be Kaeto. There was no other explanation. Kaeto, the second son with ambitions above his station, and a cruel streak that found joy in the suffering of others. If Caius were truly seen as loyal, Kaeto might reasonably assume that he would support the lawful succession. That would place him firmly in Kaeto's way. And if Kaeto saw him as an obstacle, might he secretly plot Caius' assassination?

It made more sense than any other option that Caius could see.

Caius blinked up at his ceiling, dreading the prospect of rising from his bed. He needed to take action... but what kind of action?

He could pack a bag, get on a horse, and disappear from Amarius. Maybe try to find that elusive rural idyll of which he'd been dreaming, only without the complicating factor of a male lover to court scandal among the townsfolk. It would require slipping past whatever surveillance was currently in place and evading or overpowering anyone who attempted to trap him as they'd done last night.

With planning, he was confident he could manage it. Before, he hadn't understood the nature of the threat facing him. Now, he did, and could react accordingly.

It was tempting. *Deeply* tempting.

But he knew he could never do it.

Icy rage had been gathering in his stomach since the moment the assassin had confessed to Caius being the target. Part of that rage might have been directed toward the attack on the empire's integrity. Mostly, though, it was personal. He knew if he fled with his tail between his legs in an attempt to save his own skin, that decision would curdle and fester until it ate him alive from the inside out.

After his humiliating cowardice on an Eburosi beach, Caius had vowed never to flee in the face of fear again. His life since then had been defined by his willingness to stand and fight, even against overwhelming odds. In the four years since his arrival in the capital, faced with battles that took place with words and scheming rather than swords, he'd begun to lose that part of himself.

It was time to reclaim it.

With a growl, he forced his body into motion... into compliance with his will, as he'd done so many times before. His aches and pains didn't matter. His bruises and scars didn't matter. His limp didn't matter. All that mattered was what needed to be done next.

He rolled out of bed and stripped himself of his filthy clothing from the previous night, ignoring every warning twinge of muscle and sinew as his body protested. He bathed. He dressed as befitted a respected imperial advisor. He ate the food that Tertia had left for him, strapped on his sword belt, and walked to the palace, because he was damned if he'd arrive in the back of a cart like an invalid.

On his way, he detoured to the kennels. As he approached, mournful howling could be heard emanating from the low building that housed the hounds. Pip emerged from the door just as Caius walked up.

"Decian's not here—" the lad began, sounding more than a little harried. His gaze caught on

Caius, and he cut himself off, staring for a long moment. "What in the One God's name happened to your face?" he blurted.

"Decian had to leave unexpectedly," Caius told him, ignoring the question. "Unless someone with more authority tells you otherwise, you're the new master of hounds. If you know another boy who can take on the apprentice position, hire him."

Pip gaped at him. Eventually, he seemed to come back to himself. "Is he all right, though? Decian, I mean?"

Images of bloody jaws and red, glowing eyes rose in Caius' memory. "He was, the last time I saw him." He felt physically ill as he said the words, but Pip didn't need to know about any of that. "You'll hear talk saying otherwise, I expect. Just nod and play along, and do your best to forget about him. He won't be coming back."

Pip's eyes were very wide, but after a moment's hesitation, he nodded. "If you say so."

"I do." More eerie howling echoed around the courtyard. Caius frowned. "What's the matter with the dogs?"

"Dunno," Pip said. "They've been like this since late last night." He shrugged. "Maybe they can tell he's gone an' left us."

The nauseated feeling grew worse. "You should know that it wasn't his choice to leave."

"Didn't think it was," Pip retorted.

"Congratulations on your promotion," Caius told him, and walked away.

When Caius arrived at the palace, he couldn't help but hear the pages and household servants whispering behind his back. As he approached the throne room, the imperial herald's eyes bugged — presumably because he looked like he'd come out on the wrong end of a bar brawl.

"Sir!" the flustered man protested, but Caius pushed him aside and strode into the great chamber, ignoring his impotent fluttering.

Inside, Emperor Constanzus sat upon his throne, flanked by Kaeto and Bruccias, and surrounded by buzzing courtiers. As the commotion of Caius' arrival registered, all eyes turned to him.

"What is the meaning of this?" wheezed one elderly hanger-on, who apparently had an inflated view of his own importance.

Caius strode up to the group, his uneven footsteps echoing in the vast hall.

"The master of hounds and I were attacked by half a dozen brigands last night while riding into the city for an evening of drinking," he declared, his gaze landing firmly on Kaeto to judge his reaction. "As you can see, I survived. He did not, since competence with a sword is not a prerequisite to throwing meat to a pack of dogs twice a day."

Kaeto's face might have been carved from marble. However, since it was likely that the escaped assassin had already reported back to him about the previous night's events, his lack of reaction meant little.

"I've seen to the houndsman's replacement," Caius continued. "But given the imminent commencement of the Council and the number of important persons currently lodging in Amarius, one does have to wonder about security. I would like carte blanche to deal with the situation before a diplomatic incident arises."

Kaeto raised a slow eyebrow.

Another of the officious arselickers hovering around the throne like buzzing bees raised his voice querulously. "Brigands attacking palace officials in the streets? Yes, something must be done, and quickly!"

Several other voices joined in agreement, and Constanzus waved a careless hand in Kaeto's direction. The emperor's expression was distant; Caius would have bet money that he had no real idea what subject was being discussed. Kaeto, however, knew very well what was being discussed. He offered Caius a thin smile that came nowhere near his cold eyes.

"Why, of course, Legatus," he said. "We can only thank our good fortune that you managed to escape. Speak to the palace tribuni about whatever you may need for your... *investigation*."

Caius dipped his chin in a nod. "Of course. Your Imperial Majesties..." He forced his battered body into a courtly bow, and turned on his heel with military precision, striding from the hall.

Outside, he asked around until he was successfully able to track down Jules, the pageboy who had conveyed him to his secret meeting with the empress the previous day. It seemed like a century ago.

Jules looked up from the tray of drinks he was arranging, and his eyebrows shot up in surprise. He bowed quickly, recovering his poise. "Legatus? How may I serve you today?"

Caius felt his jaw tighten, remembering his conversation with Stasia in stark detail. Her fears for the empire... her unshakeable certainty that one of her sons was plotting against her. He met Jules' eyes, knowing that his own were as hard as flint.

"I need you to arrange another meeting with your mistress for me," he said. "Tell her it's urgent."

finis

The story continues continue in *Master of Hounds: Book 2*.

For more books by this author, visit www.rasteffan.com

Made in the USA
Las Vegas, NV
29 December 2023

83606733R00152